# THE RAVEN'S CALL

Kris Humphrey

Illustrated by Chellie Carroll

**stripes**

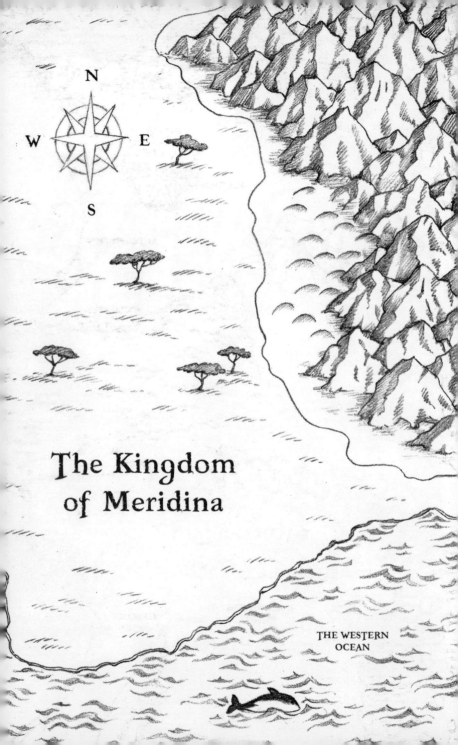

N
W E
S

The Kingdom
of Meridina

THE WESTERN
OCEAN

# CHAPTER 1

Dawn made her way slowly through the long, swaying grass. The wind seemed to fly from every direction at once, lifting her coat then pressing it against her, and tugging loose strands of hair from the braid that fell across her shoulder. Her legs felt heavy, almost as if they belonged to someone else, and the grass swished against her boots as she climbed towards the summit.

Somewhere above her, Ebony was circling. Dawn could feel her raven companion's presence between the milky layers of early morning cloud. It was as if the two of them were joined by a long, unbreakable thread, the constant closeness that only a Whisperer and her companion could experience. Even at this distance Dawn sensed what Ebony was feeling:

weariness, concentration, an exhilarated kind of fear. Ebony's sharp raven senses were already scanning the hills and valleys for demons and as soon as Dawn reached the hilltop she would do the same.

Dawn felt the familiar weight of responsibility as she climbed. As a Whisperer, it was her duty to protect the world from the Narlaw – the shape-shifting demons that had invaded and brought destruction to the kingdom of Meridina. But Dawn's duties went further than that – she was the Palace Whisperer, the leader. If she couldn't end the war against the Narlaw, then nobody could.

Sometimes the pressure made her wish she was a little girl again, back in the Southlands. She often tried to remember her childhood home – the dry warmth of the air, the herb garden and the smell of a charcoal fire at dusk. But her memories slipped away almost as soon as they arrived, extinguished by the cold grey skies. She had faced so much trouble and disaster since those days. Narlaw spies had infiltrated the palace in the capital city of Meridar, they had kidnapped Princess Ona and stolen the earthstone – an object powerful enough to rid the whole kingdom of demons. With the help of a small group of palace guards, Dawn and Ebony had pursued the demons and rescued the princess. But the earthstone was still missing. Right now, a group of Narlaw and one human traitor were carrying it south towards the waiting Narlaw army.

Dawn paused to catch her breath. She closed her eyes and let the wind roll over her. With her Whisperer senses she felt every blade of grass, every swirling current of wind. Back down the hill she felt Loren – the guard who had ridden south with her – and the presences of their two exhausted horses. She reached uphill and felt swaying trees, then dense strips of cloud that slid gracefully above it all.

*Ebony*, she whispered, sending her companion's name up into the sky.

*I'm here*, Ebony replied.

Dawn opened her eyes and saw a raven-black speck against the cloud. A smile formed on her lips as the warmth of the companion bond grew stronger. Only Ebony could force the worries from Dawn's mind. The war, the earthstone, her troubles with the king … all became manageable when Ebony was with her. Dawn watched as her companion's huge wings sailed on the twisting currents of air, descending expertly towards the hillside.

*It's hard flying today*, said Ebony as her talons gripped the shoulder of Dawn's coat. She folded her wings away briskly and shook her head.

*Did you see them?* asked Dawn.

*I saw them. When you get to the summit, you'll see them, too.*

Dawn felt a new surge of fear.

*It's all right*, said Ebony, sensing Dawn's feelings. *It's still just the three of them – and the man.*

Ebony's disgust at the human traitor was obvious and Dawn felt the same way. How could anyone take sides with the Narlaw? The whole kingdom was under threat and yet there were people willing to betray Meridina for a bit of gold.

*Three demons*, said Dawn. *That won't be easy. You saw what they did to Valderin's guards.*

The battle to rescue Princess Ona had been

short and brutal. Several of the palace guards had lost their lives and only one of them, Loren, had got through it uninjured. Captain Valderin himself had only survived thanks to Dawn's Whisperer healing and the unexpected arrival of a second Whisperer, Mika, who had headed back to Meridar with Valderin, Princess Ona and the injured survivors.

The Narlaw were so much faster and stronger than any soldier. Although they took the forms of humans, they moved like fierce hunting creatures, darting and leaping. They were almost impossible to kill. Only a Whisperer stood any real chance of defeating a demon, by banishing it back to the Darklands.

*You're strong enough*, said Ebony. *You can banish these three just like the others.*

Dawn nodded half-heartedly. *I'll do my best*, she said. If she failed to retrieve the earthstone, the kingdom would be doomed. She was too young for this, she thought. Too unprepared. The Narlaw hadn't been in Meridina for a hundred years, since they were banished by Queen Amina, the first and only Whisperer queen. No one had expected the demons to return.

As they reached the summit, a ragged line of elm trees came into view. Their branches clawed at one another and the grass beneath them was littered with leaves, autumn brown and tear-shaped. Ebony flew to perch on a low-hanging branch and pulled her wings in tight against her body, her feathers ruffling.

Dawn shivered as she peered down into the valley below. She saw the thatched peaks of several village buildings and a few patches of open ground. The rest of the valley was heavily wooded. Before the war, the morning air would have been alive with the sounds of people and animals, but now the valley was still and desolate.

*Where did you see the demons?* Dawn asked.

*On the village green,* said Ebony. *They've been there for a while – longer than they'd need just to rest the horses.*

*You think they're waiting for something?* asked Dawn as she peered down at the village green.

She could just about make out the tiny dark specks of the demons and their horses.

*Perhaps*, said Ebony. *There could be more demons on their way from Altenheim.*

Dawn stared hard at the group. Only the horses moved. The demons and their human accomplice were utterly still.

*I think you're right*, Dawn said. *They're waiting. We have to go now.* She squinted into the distance. Out there, only a few miles away, lay the rest of the Narlaw army. During the night, Ebony had flown ahead of Dawn and Loren and seen the fires raging near the city of Altenheim. She had reported back that the city itself had already been destroyed, and now the demons were marching towards Meridar. The war was escalating quickly. There were no soldiers between Altenheim and the capital, and no Whisperers either, which meant the Narlaw would march unchallenged.

Dawn looked up at Ebony and felt impatience surge through their bond.

*Yes*, Dawn repeated. *Time to go.*

When they returned to Loren, the horses were bowed over a stream, drinking, and Loren stood beside them, oiling her sword with careful strokes of a dark square of fabric. She looked up as Dawn and Ebony emerged from the trees.

"It's time," said Dawn, striding towards the copper-coloured mare that had carried her from Meridar.

Loren nodded. She was a woman of few words.

Dawn swung into the saddle and smoothed the mare's silvery mane as Ebony settled back on to her shoulder. She rode beside Loren, telling the guard what she and Ebony had seen in the valley.

"The woods go right up to the edge of the village," Dawn said, "so we should be able to approach under cover." She glanced sideways at Loren. It felt wrong to be taking charge when Loren was older, wiser and definitely more battle-hardened.

But Loren nodded in agreement. "The woods will be loud in this wind," she said. "It'll help us

14

take them by surprise."

"We have to avoid a fight," said Dawn, trying not to let her concern show. "I'll banish the three Narlaw as quickly as I can, but I need you to tackle the man they've brought with them. He'll be holding the earthstone."

"You don't have to worry about him," said Loren. She patted the pommel of her sword then spat into the grass, showing what she thought of the traitor. "These demons," she said, glancing at Dawn. "You can banish them all?"

Dawn felt her cheeks flush. "I think so," she said. If all three demons attacked her at once, she didn't know if she'd be able to cope. "It's definitely possible," she continued. "Other Whisperers have done it."

Loren nodded respectfully. "I'll help you however I can," she said.

Dawn thanked her and they fell into silence as the horses carried them through the long grass of the hillside, down towards the valley road. She watched Loren from the corner of her eye. All she'd learned during their journey was that the guard was the daughter of a seamstress, raised in the narrow, pungent streets of west Meridar, and that she had fought in the battle of Altenheim, then stepped forwards to face the Narlaw again and again. Dawn wished she could be that brave. But, deep down, she knew that fearlessness wasn't enough to save the kingdom now. Only the earthstone could do that and everyone was counting on Dawn to make that happen. She was the Palace Whisperer, a guardian of the wild. She had to do what she had been born to do.

# CHAPTER 2

Dawn peered ahead through the tangle of trees, twisting in her saddle to avoid the low, crooked branches as they went. The wind made a gushing noise in the treetops that reminded her of distant seashores.

Ebony had taken up position as scout, circling above the woodland as Dawn and Loren rode parallel to the dirt road that led to the village.

*Tell me what you see*, whispered Dawn.

*Four horses on the village green*, Ebony replied, *packed and ready to go. There's one demon and one man with them. I can see the other two demons at the far edge of the village.*

Dawn felt a surge of adrenaline. A demon on its own would be much easier to banish. And Loren would have no trouble with the human traitor. They might even get away with the earthstone before the other demons realized what had happened.

*Let me know if the other two start moving*, said Dawn.

*Don't worry*, said Ebony. *I've got my eye on them.*

Dawn kept her senses alert, scanning the woods and the road for any sign of Narlaw. Loren rode behind her, silently surveying the woods. Through the trees and across the road, Dawn spotted the first of the cottages: grey stone and a thatched roof. She reached across to the cottage with her senses and felt the rustle of mice in the thatch, but nothing else.

Dawn's stomach fluttered with nerves as they drew level with the village green. She reined in her horse, still out of sight among the trees, and let Loren pull up beside her. The green was small, with an oak tree in one corner and cottages arranged in a short line on the far side. Halfway between Dawn and the cottages stood four horses, a man and a man-shaped demon.

"The one on the right is yours," Dawn told

Loren. The man was long-haired and unshaven. He wore a knee-length leather coat and stood uneasily with one hand on his horse's saddle. Dawn studied the Narlaw that stood beside him. It had taken an old man's form, with neat white hair and the smart clothing of a country landowner. It faced away from Dawn and the woods, completely motionless – she could feel the demon taint emanating from it.

Why had they stopped for so long? If Ebony's suspicions were right, these demons were waiting for others, who were coming to secure the earthstone.

She turned to Loren. "We have to do this fast," she said. "As soon as I've banished the first demon we ride for the traitor together."

Loren nodded, drawing her sword.

Dawn closed her eyes and reached for the earth trance. Her senses immediately heightened and the woods around her seemed to burst with life. She felt the sharp taint of the demon on the green, too.

*Now*, thought Dawn. She pushed her senses out, rushing to embrace the demon. She felt it spin in panic as it realized the danger it was in.

"Go!" it ordered the man.

Dawn sensed the man leap on to his horse and felt Loren dart into motion beside her. But she had the demon. The earth flowed through her and she felt its power like a hot torrent in her veins. The demon didn't stand a chance.

She opened her eyes and saw Loren galloping across the green in pursuit of the fleeing man. The demon was gone. Three horses stamped and spun in confusion. Dawn gripped the reins of her mare and charged out of the trees, but the traitor vanished on to the wood-lined road ahead. Loren swept out of view half a heartbeat behind him. Dawn stood in the stirrups, holding on tight. There were two more demons just around that bend.

Ebony swooped low over Dawn's head. *Dawn!* she said. *More demons on the Altenheim road. Thirty at least, and they're heading this way!*

Dawn suppressed a shudder of panic and dug her heels in, willing her mare to go faster. They left the green in a final swish of grass and thumped on to the packed dirt road. Ebony raced ahead of them in a blur of deepest black and Dawn struggled to regain the calm of the earth trance as she gripped the reins and peered ahead to the next bend in the road.

*How long do we have?* she asked Ebony. *How close are the thirty?*

But a horrific wail cut through Ebony's reply. Dawn recognized the sound as a horse in distress – and it was followed by a human cry, too. Then the road curved and she thundered into a scene of total chaos.

Loren stood with her sword bared in the centre of the road. Blood trickled down her face and her horse thrashed on the ground where it had fallen beside her. Two demons stood – one in front and one behind her, their horses a short way down the road. Loren spun between the two demons with a snarl on her lips. Beyond them, the human traitor rode hard down a long, straight stretch of road.

Dawn closed her eyes and reached immediately for the demon beyond Loren. It had the form of a teenage boy, wiry and strong, and it lunged at Loren as she tried to dodge past. Dawn grasped the demon and felt sickness punch into her. She swayed in her saddle, pulling back on the reins and ignoring the second demon for the time being. The earth flooded through her and she channelled everything she could at the boy-demon.

Loren yelled as the demon reached her.

It landed one powerful strike and then was torn from the world.

Dawn opened her eyes and saw Loren scramble up and run for one of the demons' horses. In an instant she was in the saddle and charging after the human traitor. Dawn nudged her mare into a canter, but before they could move something crashed into the side of them.

The mare spun, whinnying in terror.

Dawn looked down to see the second demon leaping up – a young woman's face contorted in fury. The mare fled instinctively and the demon missed them by a finger's breadth. Dawn glanced up the road and saw no sign of Loren or the traitor. She spun her horse and they kicked off into a flat run.

*Ebony!* she called. *Stay close to Loren! Help her if you can!*

*I'm there!* replied Ebony.

Dawn rode hard. She heard the mare's breath rasp and knew this pace couldn't last for long. Behind them, the final demon sprinted in pursuit. Dawn let the mare guide them along the road and she closed her eyes, re-entering the earth trance. This time banishment felt natural, like the swinging of a blade. The demon faltered and fell – Dawn didn't need to look back to know that it was gone.

*Dawn!* came Ebony's urgent cry. *The other demons! They're here!*

*I'm coming!* cried Dawn.

She could sense from Ebony's presence that there was only a hundred paces between them. As she reached further ahead she felt a wave of darkness – the pack of demons bearing down on them. Fear trembled inside her.

"Come on!" she shouted at her mare. They had to reach the traitor before the demons did.

The hills to either side fell away sharply as the

25

dirt road carried Dawn out into a broad swathe of country where several valleys met. She saw Loren's blue cloak flapping in the wind. She saw the traitor as a dark blur just ahead. And she saw the demons, on foot, spread across an approaching crossroads.

Dawn raced, but she knew she wouldn't make it.

Seconds later the traitor reached the crossroads and merged with the Narlaw ranks.

Loren's blue cloak vanished behind him.

"No!" Dawn shouted into the wind. She felt the earth flow through her as she entered a trance. She was open-eyed and furious but the wall of evil that met her made her recoil violently.

*Where is she?* she called to Ebony. *Where's Loren?*

*She's got him!* Ebony cried. *She's found the traitor! They're right in the middle!*

Dawn saw a blur of black dart across the sky. *Don't!* she called to Ebony. *Stay back!* But Ebony ignored her, swooping towards the demons.

Dawn was close enough to see the demons' grey eyes glowing. Fifty paces ... forty ... thirty...

A flash of blue appeared.

"Loren!" Dawn screamed. She saw the guard's sword glint as it swung. She saw her stand, wrestling with the traitor as the demons clawed at her. She saw Ebony drop like a shadow between them.

Then Loren fell from her horse and was gone.

"No!" cried Dawn as she rode. She reached for the nearest demon, grasped it, fighting off the flood of sickness from the others. The earth surged and the demon flashed away to nothing. Dawn focused on the next.

Twenty paces … ten…

*Dawn!* cried Ebony. *I have it!*

Dawn broke from the trance. She looked up and saw Ebony twist into the air.

*Stop!* called Ebony. *I'm coming to you.*

Dawn reined in her mare, but the demons were already lurching towards her.

Ebony swooped down, landing awkwardly on the saddle front and Dawn grasped her companion close. Ebony shifted in Dawn's arms, cawing in pain. A heavy strip of gold fell loose from her claws – the necklace. The earthstone. Dawn glanced down.

Precious stones were set along the length of the necklace, each one the size of her thumbnail, green, blue and amber. She knew which was the earthstone instinctively. It lay in the centre – grey and cloudy like a stormy sky. She finally had it!

As soon as Dawn touched the stone her mind raced with its power. She didn't pause to think. The demons were almost on them. She closed her eyes and let the earthstone guide her, reaching out and embracing the demons as they charged. Power flowed through her and she felt the stone in her hand like a burning-hot coal. Everything turned to brilliant white, the demons as specks of darkness. Their banishment barely registered. The earthstone drove them from the world as if they were nothing. Dawn clung to the earthstone until Ebony's voice broke through.

*They're gone*, whispered Ebony. *They're gone. You can stop.*

Dawn let go of Ona's necklace and it dropped, cold and heavy, into her lap. She swayed in the saddle, opening her eyes to a world that seemed to spin and tilt around her. Her body tingled as the last of the earthstone's power ebbed away.

Ebony peered up at her from the front of the saddle. She sat crookedly, her left wing half-outstretched by her side. *We did it*, she said.

Dawn laid a hand gently on her companion's back. *Yes,* she said, *we did it.* She ran her fingers over the smooth sheen of Ebony's feathers and looked out over the crossroads. A pair of horses ran wild in the long grass, swerving at random, their reins hanging loose, but there were no demons left. The traitor was nowhere to be seen – gone into the woods, no doubt. Then, by the side of the road, she saw a blue cloak. It was Loren, lying flat on the ground, unmoving.

# CHAPTER 3

It took all of Dawn's strength to carry Loren from the battlefield. All she could manage was to lift the palace guard by her shoulders and drag her through the long grass by the crossroads, over to the trees. Dawn stood, panting for breath, and Loren lay still and silent on the mossy ground beneath a tall hornbeam tree.

Ebony hopped closer to Dawn, scattering twigs and dirt as she moved clumsily across the woodland floor. Her injured left wing hung crookedly. Dawn felt her throat tighten. Loren's face looked so strange and serene. All of her anger and determination was gone. She had given everything she had for Meridina.

Dawn fought against the onset of tears. She felt weak. The earthstone had sapped her energy in a way she'd never felt before. All she wanted was to lie down and mourn Loren's death, but a long journey lay ahead. They would have to ride back to Meridar in a wide arc if they were to avoid another encounter with the Narlaw. Dawn wasn't sure if she could banish a single demon in her present state, let alone handle the power of the earthstone another time. The stone had saved them, but it had left her vulnerable, too.

Dawn bent and picked up Loren's sword, stepping forwards to place it on Loren's body with the blade pointing down towards her feet. Then Ebony passed Dawn a slim branch of hornbeam that had fallen from the tree. Dawn tucked the branch into Loren's clasped hands, feeling how her fingers had already begun to grow cold.

*Do you remember the words?* asked Ebony, staying close by Dawn's side.

*I think so*, said Dawn. She stepped back and kneeled on the ground. The words began to surface in Dawn's mind and she placed the palms of her hands on to the damp woodland floor.

*From soil to root to branch*, she whispered. *The leaf grows and the leaf falls.*

She reached down with her Whisperer sense, into the earth, and felt it tremble beneath her. The great roots of the hornbeam tree began to rise.

*From cloud to river to sea. From the raging of the sun to the silence of the moon.*

The topsoil cracked as one thick root and then another rose up to cradle Loren's lifeless body. The tree creaked and its branches dipped as if it wished to gather Dawn, Ebony and Loren closer to it. Dawn struggled to hold her connection with the earth, shaking with effort as she watched the soil and the moss rise up and slide over Loren's legs. Vines crept around the trunk of the hornbeam tree, spreading, uncoiling and then tangling themselves in a web of green. The moss slowly rose to cover Loren's face.

*From soil to root to branch*, Dawn repeated finally. *The leaf grows and the leaf falls.*

The burial mound closed over and the vines fanned out across its length, bursting into flower in a flourish of white and blue.

Dawn bowed her head, exhausted, as the rite came to an end. She felt tears pushing at her eyes.

*Dawn*, said Ebony. *Dawn. We have to go.*

Dawn felt Ebony's feathers brush against her hand, then the smooth bony surface of her beak.

*Come on,* said Ebony.

Dawn nodded, wiping her eyes, then rose to her feet. Ebony peered up at her and it took Dawn a moment to remember her companion's injured wing. She bent down and let Ebony climb on to her hand and then up on to her shoulder.

*We'll try healing that wing of yours on the way,* Dawn said, heading towards the treeline where the horses were hitched.

The crossroads were eerily quiet as Dawn tethered Loren's horse to her own, ready for the long ride north.

Evening came, turning the clear autumn sky an inky blue. Insects spiralled around them as Dawn and Ebony charted a path that they hoped would keep them out of range of the Narlaw army. They curved west towards the mountains, which stood out like purple teeth against the setting sun. Whenever Dawn felt strong enough, she entered the earth trance and tried to heal Ebony's wing a little more – she could feel her companion's impatience like a persistent itch.

*We could be in Meridar before noon tomorrow if we pushed the horses harder*, said Ebony.

*And if they collapsed?* asked Dawn. *And if we run into more demons?*

*Then we'd deal with them*, said Ebony.

*I'm in no state to banish anything*, Dawn said. *I can barely scan fifty paces ahead.*

Ebony stretched both wings, brushing against Dawn's hair. *It's getting better*, she said. *The healing has started to work.* She tried a cautious flap and Dawn felt the echo of her companion's pain through the bond. But Ebony flapped again regardless, and kept going until she rose jerkily from Dawn's shoulder.

*Careful*, said Dawn. *You might do more damage.*

But Ebony rose and rose, sending an exultant caw out across the low grassy hills around them.

The light was fading quickly, and after a while Dawn could barely see Ebony any more. Content just to feel her companion's presence overhead, she turned her attention back to the road. There were buildings on a forested hillside up ahead. For the first time that day, Dawn's thoughts turned to food and shelter. The search for the earthstone had blocked everything else from her mind, but now she felt the creep of hunger.

For a few moments she imagined the food she would eat when she arrived back at the Palace of the Sun, then her daydreams were interrupted by a cry from above.

*They're coming!* called Ebony.

Dawn looked to the sky and saw Ebony as a dot to the south, growing larger by the second. She reined in her horse.

*Who?* asked Dawn. But there was a lead weight of fear in her stomach. She knew the answer.

Ebony swooped low. *On the valley road*, she

whispered urgently. *Two, maybe three hours behind us. A group of demons, ten or fifteen maybe, riding fast.*

*They have horses?* Dawn asked.

Ebony landed on the front of Dawn's saddle. She folded her wings with a sharp wince of pain. *Yes,* she said.

*Then we'll have to ride for it,* said Dawn.

Ebony clacked her beak and flapped into the air and Dawn kicked her mare into a gallop. Behind her she heard Loren's horse do the same.

*I've never seen horses ridden so fast,* said Ebony, landing back on Dawn's shoulder.

*How long do we have?* asked Dawn.

Ebony cocked her head, digging her claws in tight. *Three hours, perhaps. If we can keep up this pace.*

*If we can't outrun them then we'll have to hide,* Dawn said.

*And if they find us?* asked Ebony.

Dawn didn't want to think about that. *If they find us,* she said, *then we fight.*

# CHAPTER 4

Princess Ona gazed around the lavishly decorated chamber. She took in the polished tables and cabinets, the embroidered cushions, the vases, statuettes and gilt-framed mirrors. These were her things. She had grown up here. But somehow it didn't feel like home any more.

For three days and nights, Ona had been a prisoner of the Narlaw. She had been lured to the edge of the palace grounds, locked inside a cart and driven south towards the waiting Narlaw army. She had witnessed the calm, dead eyes of the demons and seen men and women die to bring her back to Meridar.

Now she looked at the luxurious rooms she had grown up in and saw how narrow her life had been.

On a polished wooden sideboard stood one of her jewellery stands. It was a porcelain tree and its branches were draped with gold chains, earrings and jewelled necklaces. But one necklace was missing – the one containing the earthstone.

She felt ashamed to have returned home while the earthstone was still in Narlaw hands – while Dawn was still out there, doing everything she could to retrieve it. Ona was a year older than Dawn, and yet she felt like a spoiled child by comparison.

She went to the windows, opening the shutters on a morning of grey cloud and cool air. Her chambers were high up in the King's Keep, the square-walled tower that stood as a fortress at the centre of the Palace of the Sun. The whole of Meridar lay before her, yellow sandstone buildings with their pitched roofs jostling for space. Ona heard the sounds of military training in the parade ground far below. She peered down and saw people marching, hundreds of boots striking the flagstones in an almost-perfect rhythm. Meridar was a city preparing for war.

In less than an hour Ona was due in the main

council chamber. She had arranged a gathering of all of the Whisperers who had made it to Meridar and, after some consideration, her father had agreed to let Ona take charge of the meeting. She had never done anything like this before and her hands began to tremble at the thought of it. She gripped the window ledge. When she and Dawn had parted, Dawn had urged her to take control of the city's defences. Both Ona and Dawn had thought the king too frail and absent-minded to lead the kingdom into war. But since Ona's return, the king had seemed much better. Ona stepped back from the window and turned to see her maid, Leah, arrive from the dressing room. Leah held up a long gown of grey velvet for Ona to inspect.

"That will be perfect," said the princess. "Thank you." She felt her voice waver and spotted a nervous look in Leah's eyes as she curtsied then hurried away. This, Ona knew, was where her only real skills lay – selecting expensive gowns from the vast collection that hung in her dressing room, matching furniture to window drapes, making small talk for hours on end.

And what else?

She couldn't fight like Captain Valderin and his palace guards. She couldn't speak with animals or summon the power of the earth like a Whisperer. She couldn't even organize or plan like the king's warden, Lady Tremaine.

Ona took a deep breath and tried to push her self-doubt aside. What she did have was the desire to change. She had survived three days in the hands of the Narlaw – surely that meant something?

Ona emerged into the corridor in her grey velvet gown and found a young girl standing sentry at her door. Since a Narlaw posing as a guard had kidnapped Ona, the king had finally agreed that it should be the Whisperers who guarded Ona's chambers, as they were the only ones who could sense a demon in human form.

The sentry turned and nodded in greeting. Ona recognized the Whisperer's free-flowing hair and her long green coat. "Good morning, Alice," she said.

"Good morning," Alice replied, nodding again. Her eyes darted over Princess Ona, examining her, weighing her up.

"You didn't bring your wolf?" said Ona as they set off together down the torch-lit corridor.

Alice glanced up at her with a confused expression, then looked back over her shoulder. Ona's heart leaped as she saw the huge grey-black creature padding a few short paces behind them. The wolf's dark fur seemed to absorb the torchlight and her eyes peered up at Ona intently. Ona turned back to Alice, embarrassment heating her cheeks, but Alice flashed her a good-natured smile. "Storm doesn't like to be seen. Even without a forest around her, she can blend in."

"She's very beautiful," Ona said to Alice. Then she turned to Storm. "You're very beautiful," she said, and Storm's golden eyes gleamed back at her.

Ona, Alice and Storm descended the stairs to the king's chambers and the sounds of furious activity echoed up to greet them. Ona heard the hushed voices of palace servants and the sharp voice of Lady Tremaine. Footsteps scurried, doors creaked and thumped.

As they reached the broad corridor that ran the length of the Keep, sunlight flooded over them through the rows of east-facing windows. A pair of young servants hurried past, bowing as they did so and keeping their polished trays perfectly level. Ona smelled fresh bread beneath the crimson cloths that covered the trays. One of the servants glanced back at Storm and Ona noticed the wolf's nostrils flare at the smell of food.

"She's hungry – it's been a long night," Alice explained. She slowed her pace and reached out a hand. Storm tilted her head and brushed against it affectionately.

At the far end of the corridor stood the tall carved-oak doors that led to the council chamber. The doors were open, allowing a constant trickle of servants to come and go. To either side of the doors stood Guards of the Sun. The memory of her abduction returned to Ona in a cold rush of fear. She forced herself to stare at the guards' red and gold cloaks. These were not demons – they were guards placed here for the protection of the king. She felt Alice's hand on her sleeve and glanced down at the young Whisperer. Alice knew the details of Ona's abduction. Everybody knew.

"Don't worry," said Alice. "There are at least a dozen Whisperers in that room. No demon could even get close."

Ona nodded. She knew she was being irrational, but fear had a way of breaking through reality.

As they neared the council chamber, Lady Tremaine emerged from a side door. She smiled at Ona, inclining her head with a deference that was also condescending. "Your Highness," said the warden. "The Whisperer council is ready to begin."

"Lady Tremaine," said Ona, with a nod.

As Ona passed the Guards of the Sun and entered the long, sun-bright council chamber it felt as if she had strayed into another world.

Around the table sat Whisperers of all ages and appearances, some chatting, some sitting quietly and some chewing on the fresh bread that had been distributed in bowls. A huge red bird flapped past Ona's head, causing her and Lady Tremaine to flinch. The bird – a parrot – landed on the shoulder of a middle-aged woman who reclined casually on one of the extra seats that had been placed around the edge of the chamber. The woman watched Ona closely, a look of wry amusement in her eyes.

Ona stood beside the warden, just inside the doors. She could see her chair at the head of the table, a quill, inkpot and small stack of paper placed there in readiness. She peered around the room – there were sixteen Whisperers in all.

The warden spoke to Ona quietly, but Ona's attention was elsewhere. She watched Alice and Storm stroll to the back of the room and join two Whisperers of a similar age. They were dressed as if they had travelled all the way from the far south. At their feet lay a leopard, its gold and black fur being groomed by a small white monkey with a streak of red down its back.

"Your Highness?"

Ona met Lady Tremaine's worried gaze.

"Your Highness," repeated the warden, "did you hear what I said? The king has confined Guard Captain Niels to the infirmary so you won't run into him. We thought that the best solution."

Ona felt a shiver of fear at the mention of that name. Niels was the guard whose form her Narlaw abductor had taken. Until now it hadn't crossed her mind that she might be confronted with his face again, but it was true – since Dawn banished the demon, the real Niels would have woken from the ghost-sleep. She mumbled a thank you to Lady Tremaine then stared across the room at a young woman whose right hand was encircled by a thin green snake. Next to her sat an elderly woman whose coat was covered in pockets and full of holes. The coat bulged as something moved about beneath the folds and Ona looked away quickly, worried at what she might see.

It was hard to tell which Whisperers and which companions went together. A wild dog the colour of sand prowled around the shaded side of the chamber. A large bat hung upside down from an unused tapestry hook. Ona wished she could relax enough to enjoy the spectacle. She glanced about and spotted a chameleon, a porcupine and a wild pig with huge curved tusks. In the far corner, near Alice and Storm, there sat a very old Whisperer. Her hands were folded patiently across her lap and at her feet sat a big cat the likes of which Ona had never seen before. Its fur was striped in silver and white and its ears tufted wonderfully above serene yellow eyes. Ona stared and stared. It was the most beautiful creature she had ever seen.

Before the princess could spot any more companions, Lady Tremaine's imperious voice rang out: "All rise for Princess Ona!"

There was a rumble of chairs and feet as the gathered Whisperers stood expectantly. Ona stared around the room, frozen in fear.

"Time to take your seat," the warden prompted her in a whisper.

Ona forced a smile, strode to the head of the table and lowered herself into the high-backed chair.

"Please sit," she said. Her voice sounded tiny

and irrelevant. The Whisperers sat quietly and Ona thought she spotted amusement twinkling in some of their faces. Her stomach fluttered with nerves, but wasn't this what she had wanted? To be taken seriously? To do her duty as a princess should?

She swallowed hard, glanced down at the quill and paper for a moment then surveyed the room and projected her voice as powerfully as she could. "I'm not one of you," she said, "but I speak on behalf of Dawn, the Palace Whisperer. She asked me to convene this council, and so I have." She paused for breath and did her best to look composed while she thought of what to say next. "Meridina is at war," she said. "The Narlaw have returned. We must work together now. We must do everything we can to defend Meridar until Dawn comes back with the earthstone."

A few of the Whisperers nodded and Ona's confidence began to grow.

"So," she said, casting her finest regal gaze around the table, "let this council of war begin."

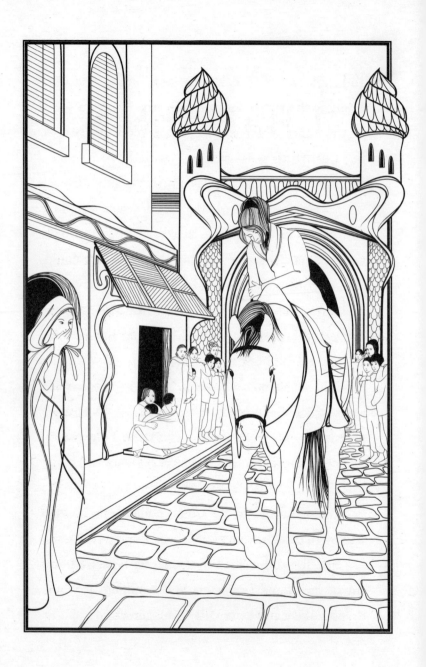

# CHAPTER 5

Once Ona had started the Whisperers talking, she sat back and followed the discussion while her pulse gradually slowed. She had never attempted to command anyone's attention like that before – let alone a room full of Whisperers.

"The question as I see it," said a woman with greying hair tied back in a long ponytail, "is how we defend an entire city with just sixteen Whisperers. We don't know when – or even if – Dawn will make it back with the earthstone. We have to be clever. We have to predict where the Narlaw will break through and be there in advance." While she spoke, the large bat that had been hanging from the tapestry hook flitted down and landed on her shoulder. Its wings draped like leather over the Whisperer's coat.

"But you're forgetting, Edie – only half of us have actually banished a demon before." This was spoken by a graceful-looking woman whose companion was the tusked boar. She had already introduced herself as Katarina. "We need to pool our knowledge," she said. "We need to teach the ones who don't know – me included."

The young Whisperer with a snake coiled around her hands spoke out. "We already know the *theory* of banishment," she said, "but you can't learn properly until you've got a demon in front of you."

"Yes," called someone else from the back, "and by then it's too late!"

Ona watched the debate fly back and forth. She saw old and young at odds with each other. She saw Whisperers sitting silently, their minds working over the problem while the others argued. She looked to the back of the chamber and saw Alice, with Storm sitting upright at her feet. A thought arrived in her head and she knew it was a good one.

"You could form into pairs," she said. Her voice was barely audible over the general noise. "Listen!"

she called out. "If you form pairs – one experienced in banishment and one not – then one can protect the other while they learn." A hush fell over the table. "You learn as you go, but not alone. Eight teams of two, spread across the city to cover the weakest points in the wall." She caught Alice's eye. "Everyone who has banished a demon raise your hand."

Six out of sixteen put up their hands. For the first time Ona noticed Mika sitting quietly by the wall with Star the arctic fox in her lap. Mika had woken Ona from the ghost-sleep and she smiled at the princess as she raised her hand. Ona smiled back. Mika looked tired and Star seemed to be sound asleep despite the noise of the council.

"So," said Ona, addressing the room as a whole, "we can have six teams to begin with. Once everyone knows how to banish, maybe you can split up?" She looked around the room. "What do you think?"

Edie tilted her head and shrugged. "Sounds reasonable."

Katarina nodded. There was a general murmur of agreement.

"That's settled then," Ona said. She looked over at Mika. "There's another thing we need to discuss," she said. "Urgently. Mika, would you like to stand and tell the council what you've discovered?"

Mika stared back at her, visibly nervous, but she rose to her feet, cradling her sleeping companion in her arms. She glanced round at the assembled Whisperers and, when she spoke, her voice was clear and deliberate. "My name is Mika," she said, nodding in greeting, "and I've found a way to wake people from the ghost-sleep."

The chamber echoed with outbursts of surprise.

"There's more!" said Mika, raising her voice to be heard. "When the sleeper awakes, the demon is banished – but not just to the Darklands – they're banished from the earth completely."

"How do you know that?" called the girl with the snake.

"You can feel it," said Mika. "The binding that traps someone in the ghost-sleep is a part of the demon. When you destroy the binding, you destroy the demon."

"Does that mean we could banish the demons for good?" asked Katarina.

Mika nodded, a shy smile lighting her features.

Ona thanked Mika over the excited murmur that echoed round the room, then she did her best to steer the debate towards a definitive plan of action. She took the paper and quill and jotted down the main points as they arose: Whisperers into fighting pairs, Mika to the front so she could test her theory right away, infirmary duty and the weak points in the city walls. She felt a thrill as she wrote and spoke out and grew in confidence at the head of the council. This was what Dawn had wanted – the Whisperers of Meridina together against the Narlaw. But for all their careful planning, the talk seemed to gravitate back to the same question: what happened if Dawn didn't return with the earthstone?

"We can hold out for as long as we like," said the girl with the snake, whose name, Ona discovered, was Seren. "But if we have no earthstone, we don't stand a chance of banishing the entire army of demons. It's impossible. Dawn must know that, otherwise she wouldn't be chasing the stone while the demons march on Meridar."

"We don't know it's impossible," said Edie. "We just know the earthstone gives its bearer incredible power. If Dawn doesn't make it, then we just keep fighting, keep banishing. What else can we do?"

Ona stayed quiet. Dawn had been clear about her opinions on this matter – there could be no final victory without the earthstone. Should she tell them this, or leave some hope that they still had a chance without it?

A Whisperer at the back of the room called out, "If Dawn doesn't return then we should link together." It was Nara, one of the young southlanders. "We did this in Altenheim," she said, gesturing to Tuanne and Lucille who sat alongside her. "The earth trance becomes more stable and you can banish more demons in one go. If the battle turns against us, we could fall back and join together at the palace. Perhaps we can survive like that – I don't know."

Ona scribbled on her paper as more questions circled the room.

*If Dawn does not return.*

Just writing those words made her feel like a traitor to her friend. Dawn had to return. She just had to.

Ona left the council chamber buzzing with excitement. The meeting had lasted almost two hours and her head was full of the stories that had been exchanged between the Whisperers – stories of hard travel and confrontations with the Narlaw; stories of daily life out on the margins of the kingdom. Ona listened, absorbed in their mystical world, watching as their companions slept or grew restless or investigated the other animals in the room. She longed to be a Whisperer, but, for now, it was enough to share a room with them.

She made sure she was the last to leave, taking careful note of each of the Whisperers' names before they left. She recited these names silently as she marched through the corridors of the Keep towards the king's private chambers. She felt exhausted, but proud. Now all she had to do was present their plans to the king.

She entered the king's reception room, bypassing her father's head clerk as he began to speak. The doors to the king's private rooms stood closed and guarded.

"Wait," called the head clerk. "You can't go in there! There's a war meeting in progress."

Ona pushed on the doors, knowing that the guards to either side wouldn't dare make a move to stop her. The clerk's voice faded, replaced from inside by the sombre tones of Captain Valderin. The captain paused and looked up as Ona entered. She noticed his stooping posture and the bandage wound tightly around his midriff. A huge map lay half unrolled on a table before him. Around the table stood her father, Magda of the Guards of the Sun and several noblemen. The room was lit by the glow of hundreds of candles.

"Daughter?" said the king. He leaned on the table with two hands and a deep frown wrinkled his forehead.

Ona instantly regretted her intrusion. She glanced from one stony gaze to the next, realizing she had strayed out of her depth. Silence stretched as she struggled to produce the words she had come here to say. "The Whisperer council is over," she managed at last. "I came to tell you what was decided."

The king rose from his leaning position and Ona saw again how the coming war had dragged her father out of his years-long spell of despondency. He stood tall, eyes ablaze in the candlelight. "Give me a moment with my daughter," he said to his captains.

Valderin, Magda and the nobles filed out in respectful silence. Ona met Valderin's gaze as he passed and caught a tiny nod of encouragement.

The doors closed behind them and the princess was alone with her father.

King Eneron stared down at the map and Ona stepped closer, seeing that it portrayed the whole of Meridar, street by street. Chalk circles had been marked around the gates in the south of the city wall. "Are these the main defensive posts?" she asked.

Her father stayed silent.

"The Whisperers need to know where to station themselves, which gates are most vulnerable. We decided—"

"The Whisperers do not *decide* anything!" bellowed the king. "*You* do not decide anything! I am king here, am I not?"

Ona looked down at her shoes, her face burning with humiliation. "Yes, Father," she said.

"What made you think you could barge into the middle of a war meeting, Ona?"

Ona shrugged. "I'm sorry," she said. "I just wanted to help." All of a sudden she felt like a little girl again.

"I understand you want to help," said the king, his voice softening to its usual low rumble. "I thought that if I let you chair the Whisperer council you'd be satisfied, but instead it's put silly ideas into your head. The defence of Meridar is not your concern. You're a good, sweet girl, but you know nothing of these matters."

Ona stared at the floor, feeling the disappointment in her father's gaze.

"You mustn't worry," the king went on. "Lady Tremaine will speak to the Whisperers. I know how important they are and we'll make sure they're welcomed into the ranks of the guards. But the best way you can help me now is to stay safely in the Keep and let me and my staff win this war."

Ona was silent. A part of her wanted nothing more than to hide away in her chambers and let the city stand or fall around her. But when she thought of the Narlaw that had kidnapped her, the people who had died to save her, her blood began to run hot. She couldn't just stand by and watch. She couldn't go back to being that pampered princess.

"It's Dawn who'll win this war," she said, looking up into her father's eyes. "Dawn and the Whisperers."

The king's face darkened at the mention of Dawn's name.

"And I know more about the Narlaw than you

or the warden," said Ona. "More than most of your generals, too. I was kidnapped by demons, I've spoken to them and seen them fight. I'm going to work with the Whisperers until Dawn comes home with the earthstone," she said. "I love you, Father, but I'm not the fragile little girl you think I am."

She turned and left before her father could reply. The doors swung behind her and the clerk gaped as she strode by. She swept past Valderin and the other captains then out into the main corridor, hurrying away, not knowing where she was going. Her heart pounded and her eyes welled with tears. The walls of the King's Keep flashed by as she raced down wide, spiral staircases, through corridors and kitchens, reception halls and servants' quarters.

Only when she stopped to look around did Ona find that she was outside, staring across the vast parade ground with tears streaking her cheeks. She wiped her face with the back of her hand and watched the latest recruits march and turn under a drill sergeant's orders. Flags rippled and snapped in the wind. The outer walls of the palace loomed like an echo of her father's commands.

Ona struck out for the busy gateway that led to the city, weaving through the chaotic ranks of soldiers and volunteers. She drew all kinds of looks and she ignored all of them, pushing on until she had passed through the gate.

Then a commotion stirred the crowds and Ona was jostled to the side of the road. She saw a tall woman striding gracefully through the parting crowd. Others followed and Ona recognized them instantly.

"Katarina!" she cried out. "Alice! Nara! Tuanne!" She struggled towards the centre of the road. She heard her name murmured around the crowd and her way became suddenly clear.

"Princess," said Katarina, bowing in greeting.

Alice smiled at Ona, and Nara and Tuanne nodded politely. The Whisperers' companions had the crowd staring in wonder and disbelief, an incredible combination of wolf, boar, leopard and monkey.

"We're heading to the South Gate," said Katarina, "to scout the defences."

"Then I'll join you," said Ona.

From the palace, King's Parade ploughed a direct line through the centre of the city, all the way to the majestic arch of the South Gate, and it had become a gathering place for people with nowhere else to go. Palace guards and city militia patrolled up and down, moving people into accommodation as it became available. Ona saw schools and warehouses crammed with refugees. She saw desperate-looking travellers shuffle into the backstreets seeking a doorway or an alley to make their own. They passed a man arguing bitterly with a militia woman, refusing to give up the shop floor of his textile factory as temporary housing.

"That'll be the least of his troubles soon," said Alice, drawing up alongside the princess. "I wonder if these people understand what's coming."

"I think they know," said Ona. "Maybe they just don't want to believe it."

They left the factory owner behind and the argument faded into the clamour of the city.

Ona noticed that Alice was staring into the distance. She tried to follow her gaze, but could only see crowds upon crowds of people.

Then Storm let out a soft, low growl. The wolf's ears stood upright as if she was scanning for something in particular.

"A rider," said Alice.

The other companions had sensed it, too. Flame the leopard edged ahead of Nara, flicking her tail. Katarina's boar snorted, and Nimbus the monkey stood upright on Tuanne's shoulder peering south down the avenue.

"There," said Nara. "A scout."

Ona finally saw it emerge from the crowds – a tall black horse trotting with a figure on its back. As the rider approached, Ona recognized the blue cloak of a palace guard. The rider sat slumped in her saddle, clutching her left arm, which hung lifeless and crooked by her side.

Katarina ran to the rider's side. "You're hurt," she said. "Let me help you."

"No," breathed the woman. "I can't stop. I have to see the king."

Ona stepped forwards, jogging alongside the

horse as it divided the murmuring crowds. "I'm Princess Ona," she said. "Tell me, what's your message for the king?"

The guard peered down at her with unfocused eyes. "The demons," she said. "They came at first light, overran our guard post on the Altenheim road. There were forty guards there, and now…"

"Where was this?" asked Ona. "How far away?"

The guard swayed in her saddle and winced as she moved her broken arm. "Four hours' ride," she said. "They came out of the fields. From all directions. We didn't stand a chance."

Ona left the guard's side and let her continue through the crowds on King's Parade. She turned and was met with grim silence from the Whisperers.

"They're coming," she said.

# CHAPTER 6

Dawn steered her horse off the main road and on to a track that wound uphill through dense woodland. Night had already fallen and the trees creaked ominously around her.

*Ebony*, she called. *Where are you?* She reached skyward with her senses. The winds swirled and, moments later, she felt her companion's presence draw near.

Ebony emerged from the pitch-black and her great wings batted the air as she landed on the pommel of Dawn's saddle. Dawn's horse ducked her head and side-stepped in surprise.

*What's wrong?* asked Ebony.

*Nothing*, said Dawn. *I just… Have you seen the demons? How close are they?*

Ebony hopped on to Dawn's shoulder and a reassuring warmth pulsed through the bond. *They're still gaining on us, but hopefully our little trick will work.*

*I hope so, too,* said Dawn.

A few miles back, at a fork in the main road, Dawn had dismounted and done her best to obliterate their horses' tracks. Now they were climbing the hill Dawn had spotted earlier. There were buildings clustered near the summit and their plan was to hide there, watching the main road from above as the demons passed them by. It was a desperate plan, but there was no way she could outrun the demons on her exhausted horse.

The path zigzagged up through a dark arch of trees. Dawn peered ahead as the first of the buildings loomed out of the thickly tangled woodland on her left. It was a long warehouse of some sort, joined to the main track by a wide loading area. Several old carts lay tilted up against the edge of the trees. The warehouse doors hung open, revealing a chasm of darkness.

*Where do you want to stop?* asked Ebony.

*Not here*, said Dawn.

They carried on until the ground levelled out. A sheer cliff face rose above the trees and the roofs of five or six buildings stood outlined against the sky.

*It looks like a quarry*, said Dawn.

*Or a mine*, replied Ebony. She took off and Dawn watched her flap on to the roof of the nearest building. *I can see the whole valley from here*, said Ebony. *It's as good a spot as any.*

*Right*, said Dawn, *then this is where we stop*. She dismounted and approached the half-open door to the building. She peered inside and saw nothing but shadow. Ebony flapped down and landed on top of the open door.

*What is it?* Dawn asked. *Demons?*

*No*, said Ebony. *Something strange… This way.* She launched over Dawn's head and Dawn followed her to the far side of the building. There was a small clearing in the woods where a pile of timber and several old metal pulleys lay clumped together.

*In the trees*, said Ebony. *Straight ahead.*

Dawn stared into the dark. The leaves shushed and the bare branches scraped, but she saw nothing.

*Use your other senses*, said Ebony.

Dawn felt the bird instantly. It was huge, even bigger than Ebony, perching low in the branches of an elm tree. She felt its eyes on her, its hooked beak and its talons.

*An eagle*, she said, stunned. *But eagles never travel this far from the mountains.*

*Not unless they have a very good reason*, said Ebony.

Dawn watched the branches of the elm tree. Now she had sensed the eagle she could just about trace its outline with her eyes.

The great bird stirred and stretched its wings. Moonlight touched golden brown feathers and a yellow beak snapped open and closed.

Dawn stood in the clearing, tense and ready for something, though she didn't know what. The lower branches swung and Dawn felt a human's presence. There was a crunch of boots and she instantly backed away.

Ebony dropped from the roof on to Dawn's

shoulder. *Let's go*, she said.

*Wait*, said Dawn.

A young man stood directly beneath the eagle. He was slim and tall, although his back was slightly stooped. He held up a leather-gloved hand in greeting.

"I wasn't expecting visitors," he said.

By his voice, Dawn guessed he was only a little older than she was.

"Is that a raven on your shoulder?" he asked.

"It is," said Dawn.

"And you're a Whisperer," the boy said. "Well now." He stepped forwards into the centre of the clearing and in the moonlight Dawn saw bright, suspicious eyes set in a long, angular face. "You're a long way from the Palace of the Sun," he said.

Dawn watched him closely, saying nothing.

The boy chuckled gently, as if he found her amusing in some way, then he forced a shrill whistle through his teeth. The eagle flapped down from its perch, displaying a mighty wingspan before landing on the boy's gloved hand.

73

"This is Titus," the boy said. "And I'm Gabriel."

"My name's Dawn," she said. "And this is Ebony."

"The Palace Whisperer and her raven," said Gabriel. "Your presence honours us." He bowed his head, but his voice was thick with sarcasm.

Dawn felt a needle of annoyance at the boy's tone. "We came here to hide," she stated bluntly. "There are demons on the road. They're tracking us and we need to rest our horses somewhere. So if you can help us, we would be very grateful, otherwise, good night to you."

The boy stared at her. "Well, I can't exactly refuse the Palace Whisperer, can I?" He nodded towards the seething forest. "Come on," he said. "I'll take you to the others."

Once Dawn had fetched the horses, Gabriel led them through a dense strip of woodland towards the towering cliff face.

"How many people live here?" Dawn asked Gabriel.

"Everyone who could make it from the nearby villages," the boy replied, not bothering to turn round. "I was just passing through. Never meant to stay, but when the demons came, all anyone could do was hide. The king certainly didn't send any soldiers to help."

Dawn wanted to tell him that a few soldiers wouldn't have made a difference against the advancing army of Narlaw, but instead she made a sympathetic noise. "They tried to call everyone into Meridar," she said.

Gabriel stopped to face her. "And what about the people who couldn't get to Meridar?" he said. "The old people and the little children. The ones who live too far away and don't have carts or fine horses like yours to carry them?" He gestured at Dawn's mare – a powerful, well-fed horse from the royal stables. Gabriel shook his head and carried on through the trees. "The king and his people don't care about the rest of us," he said.

Dawn knew he was including her in that judgement, but kept her mouth shut. She had nothing to prove to this stranger. Let him think what he wanted.

From her position on Dawn's shoulder Ebony was keeping a close watch on the eagle sitting on the boy's gloved hand. *Do you think we can trust them?* she asked Dawn. *What if they're working for the Narlaw, too? He's certainly not happy with King Eneron – or you.*

*I don't know*, said Dawn, watching the back of the boy's head as he led the way through the woods. *He's angry. But wouldn't you be? Stuck out here without protection?*

*I don't like this eagle much either*, said Ebony. *It's a bird of prey. All they do is hunt other animals.*

*I'm sure it doesn't mean you any harm*, said Dawn.

*You don't know that*, Ebony replied.

*Now you're being ridiculous*, said Dawn. *We need to hide and Gabriel can help us, so let's be nice.* Although she had to admit, the boy wasn't making things easy.

Soon they reached the cliff face. It rose above a wide arc of cleared ground that was surfaced with fine gravel. Buildings surrounded the area and there were carts and bits of machinery everywhere.

Gabriel led them towards the base of the cliff and an entranceway of some kind, sealed with what seemed to be a huge slab of rock. The entranceway looked wide enough for a horse and cart to pass through. This wasn't a quarry, Dawn realized, but a mine.

"This is where you live?" asked Dawn. "Underground?"

"The only safe place left," said Gabriel.

Just before they entered, Dawn took Gabriel by the arm, forcing him to stop and turn. "Before we go inside, you need to understand why we're here," she said. "Why the demons are after us."

Gabriel looked at her quizzically. He glanced at Dawn's hand and she removed it from his arm.

"There's a reason I'm not hiding safely in Meridar," she said. She opened her belt pouch and took out Ona's necklace, careful not to touch the earthstone. "This," she said. "This is the last thing that can stand in the way of the Narlaw. The demons stole it and I stole it back." She paused, thinking of

77

Loren and the others who had died for the earthstone. "*We* stole it back. We have to get it back to Meridar safely otherwise the demons will win and the whole kingdom will be theirs forever." She felt grief rising in her throat and from the way Gabriel's expression shifted, she knew he was beginning to understand what she had gone through.

The boy nodded once. "Come on," he said. "Let's get inside." He picked a small chunk of rock from the ground and struck it against the corner of the mine entrance. Three taps, a pause, then two more. A few seconds later the slab of rock began to move. A metallic sound echoed from inside, a clanking of gears to go with the heavy scrape of the rock.

Dawn noticed that Titus had taken up a position on the cliff face.

*Perhaps I should stay out here, too*, said Ebony, *keep an eye on the road.*

*Not scared of the mine, are you?* Dawn asked.

Ebony shook her feathers in protest. *Why would any bird want to go crawling about undergound?* she said.

Dawn nodded, smiling. *You're right*, she said. *Just let me know what the demons do when they reach the fork in the road.*

*Of course*, said Ebony, flapping across the open ground to the top of a nearby oak. *Be careful in there.*

*I'll be fine*, said Dawn.

Despite the boy's spiky attitude towards her, she was certain Gabriel wasn't a threat. He was rude, but sincere. And if the people here were working with the Narlaw, why would they be hiding inside a mine?

The entrance was open now and a covered paraffin lamp spilled yellow light over the beginnings of the tunnel and the bulky frame of a woman. The woman tensed when she noticed Dawn, but Gabriel nodded at her and she stepped aside to let them in.

Dawn led the horses into the tunnel, their hooves striking loudly on the stone floor. Then the mine entrance began to rumble shut behind them. Dawn turned to see a rusted chain-and-pulley mechanism at work. A young man dressed in a dirty white shirt worked a huge metal handle with all of his strength.

He stared blankly at the newcomers, gasping with the effort of hauling the stone door shut. A hand cart lay near the entrance, stacked with empty woven baskets. For gathering food, perhaps? Dawn wondered how several villages of people managed to survive underground. There would be many mouths to feed, and scavenging outside would be very risky.

Gabriel and the woman led them further inside. The tunnel was high enough for the horses to walk through, though Dawn's mare flicked her head uneasily as they passed through pools of lamplight and eerie stretches of near-darkness. Dawn stroked the mare's nose, straining to hear as Gabriel and the woman muttered to each other up ahead. At one point, the woman turned to look back at Dawn. Her gaze was cold, and Dawn could tell the woman was judging her unkindly.

"How long have you been here?" she called ahead to Gabriel and the woman.

The woman eyed Dawn for a moment before responding. "Two weeks," she said. "Two weeks and two days."

Dawn increased her pace so she could catch up, but neither the woman nor Gabriel seemed interested in a conversation. Dawn carried on regardless. "Are you in charge here?" she asked the woman.

"I'm one of the village elders," she said. "But now it seems I'm an elder without a village." She looked sharply at Dawn. "This mine is all we've got. Everything we could carry we brought here. And if the demons find us… If you've led them here…" Her eyes were full of desperate anger.

Dawn looked down at her feet, unable to hold the elder's gaze. "I'm sorry," she said. "I've brought trouble to you and your people." She looked up. "But I really had no choice. The safety of the whole kingdom depends on my journey back to Meridar. If you can shelter us, let us rest here for a while, then you'll be doing a true service to Meridina."

The elder nodded and gave Dawn a rueful smile. "We'll do our best," she said.

They walked on without speaking. The horses' hooves scraped loudly on the tunnel floor. Several tired-faced people passed them, each busy at the work of survival. One man they overtook was dragging a vast bundle of firewood. A young woman passed them in the other direction, hefting two large pails of sloshing liquid that smelled so dreadful Dawn had to cover her face. They reached a junction in the tunnel and stopped. It was a crossroads, with two much narrower tunnels leading off to the right and left. Under the elder's lamplight Dawn could see the way ahead was barricaded by a heavy wooden structure that could have been part of a barn door.

"It's only us," called the elder, rapping against the wood with her knuckles. As the barricade slid to the side she jerked her thumb backwards to signify the new arrivals. "A traveller," she said.

A tall, stocky man peered out, taking in Dawn and the horses with a quick dart of his eyes. "Well, you'd better come in then," he muttered.

Beyond the barricade, the walls of the tunnel were lit with flaming torches and Dawn could hear a low hum of voices up ahead. She followed close behind Gabriel and the elder woman and they soon emerged into a wide chamber whose ceiling rose eight or ten paces above Dawn's head. The room was well lit and alive with activity. People sat on benches and stools, fixing clothes or carving wood or just talking. A goat was being milked in one corner of the chamber and there were two cooking fires side by side in another.

"You'll be hungry," the woman said, leading Dawn towards the fires, and Dawn suddenly realized she was.

"The horses need food more than I do," she replied. "If you have anything, I'd be…"

"Stefan!" the elder barked, cutting Dawn off. "Stefan! Come and take care of these horses!"

A boy of about eight or nine broke off from a small group of other children and sprinted over. He took the reins from Dawn with a serious look on his face. Dawn could tell he didn't want to displease his village elder – and she understood why. The woman was fearsome.

Dawn thanked him and continued towards the cooking fires, her stomach twitching in anticipation.

Gabriel was already there, bent over a small round pot and muttering to an elderly couple who seemed to be in charge of the food. She glanced to her right and saw the boy, Stefan, leading the horses through a crooked archway and into a separate chamber. The place seemed well organized. She saw stacks of firewood, vegetables in sacks and a few neat piles of hunting equipment.

Gabriel handed Dawn a bowl of steaming-hot broth and she sat beside him on a long bench. The broth smelled of salt and herbs, and Dawn's hunger must have been obvious because Gabriel flashed her a knowing smile – the first she had seen since meeting him.

"Thank you," Dawn said. "I can't remember the last time I ate anything."

Gabriel nodded. "The demons took our village by surprise," he said. "Up in the western mountains. Me and Titus left with barely a day's food and there was no time to stop and hunt. It took us seven days to get here and there were times I thought I might starve."

"But you made it," said Dawn.

Gabriel smiled again, but his eyes were full of sadness. Dawn wondered who and what he had left behind in the mountains.

"So you can stomach the broth?" he asked her.

Dawn nodded, taking another spoonful into her mouth.

"It's the best us simple folk can do," said Gabriel. "I suppose things are very different in the Palace of the Sun... It would be pheasant or duck in that soup instead of carrots and potatoes." The mocking edge had returned to his voice and Dawn looked up from her bowl, meeting Gabriel's gaze defiantly.

"I grew up in the Southlands," she said. "In the mountains where the soil is as dry as sand. Life was difficult. But life is difficult everywhere. Even in Meridar. You're not the first person in the world to have a hard time." She took another mouthful of broth and an awkward silence stretched between them. Dawn put all her energy into eating. The food was delicious and it warmed her throat and stomach. Soon her spoon was scraping the bottom of the bowl. She looked up to see Gabriel smiling at her. When she raised an eyebrow he shook his head and laughed.

"Come on," he said. "I'm sorry for getting at you. Let's start again." He held out his hand.

Dawn narrowed her eyes, then smiled despite herself. "Fine," she said, shaking his hand. "We'll start again."

"Now," said Gabriel, springing to his feet. "Let me give you the grand tour."

The mine was a labyrinth of tunnels. Gabriel led Dawn through some of the passages that branched directly off the main chamber and it was frightening how quickly she lost all sense of direction. Some of the tunnels were lit with torches or paraffin lamps strung up at long intervals. Others were utterly dark. Dawn strode quickly to keep up with Gabriel and the pool of light from the lamp he carried. They passed storerooms full of barrels and mining tools, a junction of tunnels where one branch had collapsed into rubble. Gabriel showed her a working pit face – a vertical wall of rock from which seams of coal had been gouged out by the miners. Dawn stared up at the rock. There was barely room to turn around, let alone swing a pickaxe. She tingled with claustrophobia, the need to get out into the open air becoming almost unbearable. But as they made their way back to the warmth and light of the main chamber, Dawn felt her nerves settle and she found she had a new respect for the people around her. They seemed relaxed, almost happy to be undergound, locked inside the hill by their stone doors and wooden barricades.

Dawn sat on the floor beside the cooking fires, her back against the long bench. She stayed that way for an hour or more, simply resting, listening to the sounds of the mine with her eyes half closed. She felt her eyelids grow heavier and the warmth of the cooking fires wrap around her. She knew she needed to stay awake, but her body was so tired there seemed like nothing she could do to fight it.

In the end it was Ebony who grabbed her from the edge of sleep. *Dawn!* she whispered from her perch outside the mine. *They're coming. The demons followed our trail. They know we're here.*

Dawn scrambled to her feet with a gasp, toppling the bench behind her. Heads turned to look and she stared back, barely able to register what Ebony had told her. *The demons?* she asked. *Where are they?*

*Just passed the fork in the main road,* said Ebony. *If we're going to run, we have to go now.*

*But we can't outrun them,* Dawn replied. *Our horses are tired. We're tired. There has to be another way.*

Dawn stood beside the fallen bench, weary and afraid. Did she have enough strength left to fight these demons?

*We need a new plan,* she said to Ebony, peering around the chamber at the people who had taken her in. She was looking for Gabriel and, when she spotted him, he turned and met her gaze. He seemed to know immediately that something was wrong.

*Can you keep watch for me?* Dawn whispered to Ebony. *Let me know how long we've got?*

*You know I can do that,* said Ebony.

Even through the hillside that separated them, Dawn felt the fearless determination of her companion. It gave her strength – the strength she would need to tell the people of the mine that she'd led the Narlaw to their door.

"Send her outside!" yelled a gruff young man. "It's her they want, so send her out!"

Dawn glanced from face to face. There were cries of agreement, jeers of protest. People glared at her. Some shook their heads and some stayed still and silent. Dawn had quietly informed Gabriel and the village elder about the coming Narlaw, hoping to avoid a panic. But, as the three of them had tried to form a plan, the news had spread around the small community and brought the people together.

"Quiet!" demanded the elder. She stood in the centre of the circle, close to Dawn, but not so close as to suggest she was on her side. "I said quiet!" she called again. "Since when have we conducted ourselves in this kind of rabble?"

The angry voices dwindled to a murmur and the elder gazed around sternly. Dawn could see the power this woman held here.

"This mine has been our sanctuary more than once," she said, looking up at the rough-hewn ceiling with pride. "Whenever our villlages have been threatened by lawlessness or disease, we've sheltered here inside the hill."

Dawn felt her heart lurch. Why should they give their safety up for her? She was a stranger to them, nothing more. She knew what the elder would say next. Dawn would be sent outside, just her and Ebony against the demons.

But the elder's words took a different direction.

"Never once," she said, "have we left an innocent person stranded outside this mine. Never once have we failed to help somebody who needed it." She glared around the circle of people, causing some to hang their heads, some to nod grimly.

Dawn caught Gabriel's eye and noticed the smile forming on his lips.

"This girl needs our help," said the elder. "The kingdom needs our help. And we're damn well going to give it. Now, look lively," she bellowed.

"Let's move the livestock out! Load the food and weapons. I want those carts outside in thirty minutes!"

The people went to work dismantling their temporary home. Dawn turned to thank the elder, but she had already marched off to oversee the evacuation. Instead Gabriel stood there with an eager look in his eyes.

"I think I've found a way," he said. "The mine. We can use it. We can trap them."

"What do you mean?" asked Dawn. Her mind was so tired that she could barely think.

"I mean we can lure them in," said Gabriel. "You have something they need, right? They'll have to come inside and then we escape and seal the mountain."

Dawn squinted across the cavern. "But how do we do that?" she asked. "There are ten demons at least. They'll break through anything we put in their way."

Gabriel shook his head, full of nervous energy now. "No, they won't," he said. "Not if we collapse the tunnels. These people are miners. They can do that. I know they can."

Dawn pushed aside any doubts she had. There were simply no other options. "Let's do it then," she said, "because we're running out of time."

Within seconds Gabriel had darted across the cavern and was talking to the village elder. The woman glanced over at Dawn. Her scowl was unmistakable, but she nodded nonetheless.

# CHAPTER 7

Beyond the confines of the mine the night stretched away, fresh and alive. Dawn stood beside the entrance and watched as the village elder led her people into the trees. Goats, sheep and horses trailed after them, strung on a long line of rope. Dawn's guilt at compromising their hiding place rekindled inside her. She watched as the last of them slipped into the trees.

Ebony soared high above the hillside, swooping towards the valley road in an effort to be seen by the approaching group of Narlaw.

*Twelve*, said Ebony. *They're coming in single file now, up the hill track.*

*Make sure they come to us*, said Dawn. *I don't want them going after the mine people.*

*Don't worry*, said Ebony. *I'm sure they only have eyes for you.*

Beside Dawn stood Gabriel and the big man from the barricade. Everyone else had gone, leaving them two small barrels and two storm lamps. The barrels had wicks of paraffin-soaked string poking out of their closed lids. Inside was an explosive compound that would bring any tunnel in the mine crashing down.

"You're sure you know how to light the fuse?" Gabriel asked the man.

"Same as lighting anything," the man said.

"Wait until all the demons have passed," said Gabriel, "then sprint for the exit, understand?"

"I won't be hanging about," the man said.

Ebony swept down, flapping to a hover above the small group. *They're almost here*, she said. *I think it's time to get inside.*

Dawn turned to Gabriel. "It's time," she said.

"Right," he replied. "Let's get the first barrel hidden."

Without the noise and movement of the mine-dwellers, the tunnels felt completely different. Gabriel's lamp was a bubble of light that seemed to be the only thing keeping the hillside from tumbling down to crush them. Dawn trod carefully. She heard the big man's footsteps close behind her. He had his own lamp, giving Dawn an extra shadow on the damp rock walls.

"Here," said Gabriel. He stopped, holding his lamp up to illuminate the crossroads that had been barricaded when they'd first arrived. Now the barricade was gone, ready to let the demons into the heart of the mine. "Set your powder barrel next to this strut."

"Got it," said the big man.

"Good," said Gabriel, grinning. "Then we'll see you on the other side."

The man nodded grimly.

"Thanks," said Dawn.

The man entered the side tunnel, wreathed in the glow of his lamp. Three steps later he had vanished around the corner.

Dawn and Gabriel hurried back to the mine entrance.

*Ebony*, said Dawn. *How long?*

A flash of black crossed Dawn's vision. It was Ebony. But with Gabriel's lamp so close, she could barely see five paces out into the dark. Suddenly Ebony's claws were clinging to her shoulder and the bond was pulsing with urgency.

*They're here!* said Ebony. *And they definitely saw me.*

Dawn peered out towards the hill track. She heard a thud, then another, then the clatter of hooves like heavy rain. *Fly!* she whispered to Ebony.

Her companion took off into the night.

"Are you ready?" she asked Gabriel.

He snorted nervously. "Yeah," he said, "I reckon I am." There was a screech overhead and he raised his gloved hand to Titus.

The horses trotted into view. Above them, twelve glowing sets of eyes seemed suspended in the night.

"Go!" she said, and Gabriel darted into the mine.

She picked up her powder barrel and waited two, three, four seconds, glaring at the demons until she was sure they had spotted her. Then she ducked into the tunnel, sprinting to catch up with Gabriel.

At the side tunnel Dawn glanced left. There was no sign of the big man's lamp, but there was no time to look further. She heard the echoed scrape of hooves outside and raced onwards.

"They're coming!" she hissed at Gabriel.

The tunnel boomed with footsteps.

Gabriel cursed and the lamp swayed madly as he found an extra burst of speed. His long legs carried him away from Dawn and she pushed faster, afraid of being left behind. Then the bubble of lamplight bloomed as they emerged into the vast main cavern.

"This way!" called Gabriel.

Dawn followed, diagonally across the cavern, and ducked inside another tunnel, close on Gabriel's heels.

This one was narrower than the first. Dawn's boots hit chunks of stone and she stumbled, shouldering the wall to stay upright as her tired hands clutched the powder barrel. The noise of their footsteps blanked out everything. She couldn't tell how close the Narlaw were behind them. "Will they follow us in?" she asked, breathlessly.

"It's the only way through," said Gabriel. His voice rebounded eerily off the tunnel walls.

Then he stopped suddenly and Dawn ran into the back of him. They fell together, against the stone face of a wall. Dawn struggled to keep the powder barrel from falling and Gabriel placed a hand on her shoulder to steady her.

"The junction," he wheezed.

Dawn looked around. The tunnel split off in three directions – left, right and straight ahead.

"We'll put the barrel here," said Gabriel, glancing back the way they'd come.

Dawn placed it where Gabriel showed her, tight against one of the vertical wooden supports at the centre of the junction. Now they'd stopped running she could hear muffled footsteps back towards the cavern. She looked at Gabriel, who was listening intently.

Dawn listened, too, and panic rose in her throat. What if the first explosion failed? What if the big man had been caught by the Narlaw, or run away? She glanced at Gabriel. "I—"

The tunnel shook with the force of the explosion and a wave of air blasted from the direction of the cavern. Grit rained down from the roof and an echoed boom rolled like thunder, over and over again. The support struts groaned and Dawn clutched the wall, expecting the ceiling to fall at any moment. But the tunnel held and the sound of the explosion echoed down to nothing.

"That would be it then," said Gabriel. "You ready?"

"I'm ready," said Dawn.

Gabriel bent and lit the wick. There was a bright white fizz of flame.

"Come on," he said, darting down the left-hand tunnel.

The tunnel was long and straight. Dawn grimaced as she pushed her legs harder and faster, waiting for the blast that would knock her off her feet and bring the whole world down on top of her.

Gabriel skidded to a stop. He cursed loudly. "We missed the turning!"

Dawn stopped and spun.

The lamp glowed on a tiny crawl space in the tunnel wall. Gabriel dropped to his knees and shuffled inside. "Quick!" he said.

Dawn's heart lurched. She could see two grey eyes glowing back at the junction and she felt a stab of sickness in her gut as the Narlaw came towards her.

"Come on!" screamed Gabriel.

His lamplight was almost too far ahead to see.

Dawn scrambled after him on her knees.

The lamp flashed ahead of her but she could feel the demon closing in.

She lay on her back, reaching for the earth trance.

Gabriel cried out her name, but his voice seemed miles away.

Then the powder charge blew.

Dawn screamed as something heavy fell from the ceiling, grazing her leg. More rocks clattered to the ground. The tunnel was caving in!

She scrambled backwards, pushing with her heels and scraping the walls with her fingers. The explosion echoed on and on. Her head throbbed and she saw nothing but black. Black everywhere. She spun and felt a shooting pain in her leg. She crawled forwards on her knees.

"Gabriel!" she shouted. "Gabriel!"

There was no answer and no lamplight.

Behind her, she felt no demons either.

She pushed onwards, suppressing the urge to scream. She called Gabriel's name again and, this time, there was an answer, quiet and remote.

"Here…"

Dawn crawled on, feeling the ground slowly rise. Her knees and her bare hands scraped the floor. She felt moisture low down on her left leg and knew from the sharp sting that she was bleeding.

"Dawn?"

"It's me," she breathed. "It's me."

Although she couldn't see him, Gabriel's presence was right there beside her.

"You made it," he said.

She could tell from his voice that he was grinning.

"Come on," he said. "It's not far."

The lamp had gone out so they crawled in the

pitch-black, Gabriel pausing from time to time to make sure they were going the right way. Dawn welcomed these pauses, breathing the dusty air and lying flat on the rocky ground.

She smelled the outside before she saw it. Fresh air wafted down the tunnel and Dawn greedily drank it in. Gabriel crawled ahead, grunting as he pushed clods of earth aside, and Dawn crawled after him with every bit of strength she had. She pushed her head and arms through the opening, bursting out into the night.

They set off before the sun had cracked the horizon. Dawn rode downhill on her copper mare, Ebony on her shoulder. Dawn had said goodbye to the mine-dwellers, thanking them with a deep apology in her eyes. When she'd asked their leader what they planned to do now, the woman had given her a grim smile. "Survive," she'd said. And Dawn believed that they would.

Halfway down the hillside Ebony took to the

sky. *There's someone following us*, she said.

*Demons?* asked Dawn, her heart leaping in fear.

*No*, said Ebony, with a touch of amusement. *Not demons.*

Dawn wheeled her mare around to see Gabriel trotting down the hill track behind them on Loren's horse. Titus hovered above the trees, dipping and rising on the air currents.

"I thought you could do with some company," said Gabriel as he drew near.

Dawn frowned at him, but couldn't quite keep the smile from forming on her lips. "It's a long way to Meridar," she said, "and dangerous. Are you sure you're up to it?"

Gabriel laughed and walked Loren's horse on down the hill so that Dawn had to catch up. "I've already saved your skin once," he called back.

Dawn shook her head. *How does the road look?* she asked Ebony.

*It's all clear for now*, she said. *Time to go home.*

"Home," muttered Dawn. For the very first time she found herself thinking of Meridar and the

Spiral Tower as her home. She nudged her horse into a canter, hooves drumming on the road as Gabriel matched her pace.

In its pouch, the earthstone swung and thumped as Dawn carried it north, to war.

# CHAPTER 8

Somewhere behind a veil of white cloud the sun was rising. Ona looked up through the window of the carriage, rocking to the clatter of the wheels as the driver steered them through the winding streets of Meridar towards the Outer Town – the ramshackle district that clung to the outside of the city wall. Everything was quiet and wisps of fog hung between the buildings.

Ona had spent the previous day examining the city's defences with Alice, Nara and the other Whisperers. They had walked along the south-facing city wall, meeting palace guards and militia leaders, familiarizing themselves with the defensive layout and choosing positions for each of the fighting pairs of Whisperers. It had made Ona proud to walk alongside the Whisperers and their companions, and to see the hard work going on in every crooked corner and alleyway.

When she had returned to the King's Keep, she had found Lady Tremaine waiting for her in her chambers with a message from the king: Ona was to remain in the Keep. She had been kidnapped once before and the king was adamant that nothing like that should happen again. Ona had listened politely and nodded in a non-committal way. But her father's demands felt arrogant and she had no intention of following them.

And so she had left the palace at dawn, hooded and anonymous, using the same stable-yard gate the Narlaw had taken her through at the very start of her abduction. The sight of that yard had made her stomach twist, but it was the only secluded exit she knew.

The carriage lurched to a halt and Ona grasped at the leather strap beside her to keep from flying off her seat.

"The East Gate, madam!" called the driver.

Ona fumbled in her purse as she climbed from the carriage. She paid the driver and turned to see a small square that was already busy with movement. All around the square were palace guards and militia volunteers. The soldiers chewed on lumps of bread or sipped tea from metal tins.

Deep down, Ona knew she had no business here. Although she had news for Alice and Katarina in the Outer Town, she could easily have sent a messenger instead of coming herself. But she wanted so badly to be part of the Whisperers' lives and the thought of hiding away in the Keep brought on a desperate panic.

The guards clustered around the gate eyed Ona suspiciously as she approached. When she threw back her hood it took them a moment to stand to attention and offer her the customary greetings.

"Your Highness," the sergeant said. "Forgive us. We weren't expecting you."

"I have urgent business with the Whisperers in the Outer Town," she replied. "Would you kindly let me through?"

The sergeant was a thick-set man with grey stubble on his chin. He glanced sideways at his fellow guards. "The Outer Town?" he said. "But you know we're on full alert, Your Highness? The demons were sighted on the plains. Are you sure you should be—"

"Yes," Ona interrupted. "Quite sure. Now would you show me through, please?"

The man spun on his heel and marched quickly towards the gatehouse. The main gate was closed and barricades were being constructed. Ona looked at the ancient wood of the gates and wondered how long they would stand against an army of demons.

The sergeant led her to a small door in the corner of the gate. Ona nodded her thanks and ducked through. The sergeant followed her.

"I'll escort Your Highness, if you will permit?"

"Very well," said Ona. "Until I reach the Whisperers."

The Outer Town was eerily empty. Fog curled through the tangle of unpaved streets, round buildings that were mostly wood and rarely more than one storey high.

"This way, Your Highness," said the guard sergeant. He pointed through a small stone arch that spanned the gap between a pair of low buildings. Through the arch was a courtyard about ten paces across. Colourful awnings stretched from the outer walls and were propped up on poles. It looked like a market square, but where the stalls should have been were now stacks of crates, arrow quivers and a row of swords beside a sharpening wheel. Through openings in the walls Ona saw candle-lit rooms with bunks and tables.

The sergeant looked around. He was about to barge into the sleeping quarters when a large grey-black wolf emerged from a room on the opposite side. The sergeant stopped in his tracks.

Ona smiled. "Storm!" she said.

The wolf observed her closely as she hurried over.

"Thank you, sergeant," Ona called over her shoulder, as she ducked beneath a gold and white awning. "I'll be fine from here."

"Princess?" said Alice, looking up from the apple she was cutting. "What are you doing here?"

Ona smiled awkwardly. "I have an urgent message," she said. "Where's Katarina? Is she still in the Outer Town?"

Alice laid her apple and knife on the small table beside her. "Yes, she's still here," she said. "Out on patrol with some of Valderin's guards. Has there been a Narlaw attack?"

"No," said Ona, suddenly much less sure of the urgency of her message. "I overheard the warden talking back in the Keep. They're going to set fire to the whole of the Outer Town. Burn it to the ground, so the Narlaw can't use the buildings for cover or to get over the walls."

Alice frowned. "Those orders haven't reached us," she said. "Are you sure?"

"Of course I'm sure," said Ona. "The king and his captains have only just decided on it. I came because I didn't know if the guards would tell you. You know how my father is. I couldn't bear to think of you and Katarina and the others left out here when the other

114

soldiers were pulled back behind the wall."

Alice smiled. "Thank you," she said.

But Ona could read the look in the young Whisperer's eyes: confusion and concern. Ona turned away, pretending to look through into the courtyard. She felt embarrassed, sneaking down here in childish defiance of her father.

In the doorway, Storm's ears twitched and the wolf rose to her feet.

Ona looked between Storm and Alice, certain that the pair were whispering.

Someone yelled nearby and Alice rushed out into the yard. There was a harsh clang of metal on stone then more shouting, surprised and scared. Boots thumped down the nearby streets.

"Stay here!" said Alice, shooting Ona a serious look. She and Storm ran from the courtyard and Ona was left alone.

The fog deadened all sound. There was no echo. Ona stood utterly still in the centre of the room. Then she heard what she realized must be a house collapsing – it couldn't have been more than two streets away. More cries flew into the fog-choked air: cries of fear, orders and calls for help. Ona went to the doorway and gripped the wooden frame.

The demons had come.

Across the courtyard she saw a young man peering out of his bunk room. He glanced at Ona and, seeing her, he stepped back inside. Seconds later, he emerged nervously clutching a sword and wearing a green militia tunic. He walked and then jogged out towards the rising clamour of battle. He was barely older than the princess and she was certain that if she hadn't been there to see him, he would have stayed hiding in the courtyard, just like she was.

The din of battle grew closer and Ona's heart was pounding hard. She wished she'd stayed in the palace after all.

Then a horrible cry split the air, followed by the splintering of wood. Boots pounded on the nearby streets. Ona saw a shadow beneath the archway. It stopped and turned. Ona knew instinctively it was a demon. Had it seen her? She stepped backwards, scanning her surroundings for a way out, but she was trapped.

Suddenly Storm's furious snarls filled the air and Ona watched in shock as the demon fell to the ground under the wolf's attack. Seconds later the demon vanished and Alice was standing in the archway, breathing hard.

"Come on," she said. The impatience in her voice was hard to miss.

Ona hurried from the courtyard and joined Alice and Storm, jogging against a tide of palace guards and militia, back towards the East Gate. The soldiers ran past, their faces anxious and exhausted. Ona thought of the young recruit in the courtyard. What had happened to him? Another thought struck her.

"Where's Katarina?" she asked Alice.

"She went back behind the city walls through the Drover's Gate." Alice strode ahead, leading them in a direct route to the East Gate.

Storm carved a path for them and they hurried through the soldiers thronged around the gate. When Ona looked up at the inside of the formidable city wall, she felt relief like never before.

"I shouldn't have come," she said to Alice. "I'm sorry."

Alice nodded, then smiled. "You were only looking out for us," she said. "It was good of you."

Ona smiled back, half-heartedly. "So, this is the beginning," she said, looking around the square at the swarms of soldiers readying for battle.

"The Narlaw are testing our defences," Alice said, peering up at the East Gate. "Small groups, probing, seeing what we're made of. When they come in force, we'll know it."

A cart trundled down into the square and Ona, Alice and Storm moved to let it through, pressing in close to all the waiting soldiers. The cart was laden with tar barrels and torches of dry grass.

"It looks like you were right," said Alice. "They're burning the Outer Town."

Ona watched the cart creak to a halt. A round, bald man with thick arms jumped down from the driver's seat and a younger man leaped down nimbly beside him. Ona recognized the younger of the two immediately.

"Yusuf!" she shouted.

The merchant's son craned his neck, scanning the crowd of soldiers in confusion.

Ona waved and Yusuf finally saw her. He pointed to the western edge of the square and he and Ona wound through the gathered soldiers to meet.

"I heard you were back," said Yusuf. He looked embarrassed. "I tried to see you but the Guards of the Sun wouldn't let me into the Keep."

Ona nodded. Yusuf had been a victim of the Narlaw, too. One of them had placed him in the ghost-sleep and used his form to sneak into the palace and sabotage the water supply. Even though his innocence had since been proved, he was still viewed with distrust by the king and Lady Tremaine.

"So, you've joined the militia?" said Ona, changing the subject.

"Meridar needs all the volunteers it can get," he said. "There aren't enough trained guards to defend a city of this size." He looked at her curiously. "What brings you to the East Gate, anyway? We're about to set fire to the Outer Town – but you must know that already."

Ona blushed. She saw Alice and Storm making their way closer through the crowd. "I came to deliver a message," she said.

Yusuf turned and nodded to Alice in greeting, glancing down at the huge grey-black wolf who stood beside her. "I know it's not my place to say it," he said to Ona, "but you should look after yourself. You'll be queen one day and the kingdom needs you. You shouldn't be risking your life on the front line."

"I know," said Ona, glancing at Alice. "I just needed to help. My father wants me locked away in the Keep, but I can't sit by and do nothing. I just can't."

The cart driver called to Yusuf gruffly.

"I have to go," he said. He smiled at Ona. "There are other ways to help defend the city," he said. "You're our princess. The people love you. They'd do anything you tell them to do." With that, he jogged away, back to the cart.

Ona and Alice silently left the square, walking

uphill against the dwindling flow of militia and guards. The sun was a white circle in the cloudy eastern sky and the final strands of fog hung in the backstreets, ready to be burned away by the coming day. All around, the people of Meridar woke, opening their doors to begin their first morning in a city under siege.

# CHAPTER 9

Ona stood alone on the roof of the city customs house. She leaned against the sandstone battlements and looked east to where the Outer Town burned. She had hurried through the city with Alice and Storm, all the way to the docklands and the customs house, where Alice had left her. It was a relatively safe place, and Ona was glad not to have been sent back to the palace.

The customs house had become a militia command post. On the ground floor, refugees queued with their belongings, seeking shelter in one of three floors above. All but the very frailest people had to be turned away. Ona had toured the building, greeting the volunteers and the refugees, looking for a chance to help. But the volunteers just smiled, not taking her offers seriously. She saw families clustered in the hallways, people asleep in storage cupboards and beneath desks. Few of the refugees had proper bedding and Ona saw the meagre bowls of food that were handed out from the makeshift kitchens. It was barely enough to keep a person alive. Everyone she asked said the same thing: no more space, not enough food. Eventually Ona had found the clock tower and its square of flat rooftop.

A northerly wind rolled down off the hills. The morning fog was gone, but in its place rose a dreadful shroud of smoke that billowed from the Outer Town. The city wall wasn't far from where Ona stood and she could see the outlines of the soldiers on its battlements. To the east, the arch of the South Gate loomed against the clouds of smoke. Much closer, Ona pinpointed the Stonecutter's Gate then the River Gate directly south of her. These were the weak points in the city's defences and, like the king's soldiers, the Whisperers had spread themselves evenly between them. Alice had gone to join Nara and Tuanne at the Stonecutter's Gate.

Ona looked down at the river and the busy docklands, following that gleaming ribbon of water to where it exited the city through the vast iron portcullis of the River Gate. A great raft of barges had been anchored there, each of them alive with the movement of troops.

The roof hatch thumped open behind her and Ona turned, expecting to see a Guard of the Sun arriving to escort her back to the palace. But it was Yusuf who clambered through the hatch. He glanced up and smiled as he saw her.

"How did you find me?" called Ona.

Yusuf lowered the hatch and came towards her. "I asked around," he said. "You'd be surprised how many people noticed their future queen striding through town with a Whisperer and a huge grey-black wolf."

Ona smiled. Yusuf had a gift for cheering her up.

"So, you finished at the Outer Town?" she said, pointing towards the rising plumes of smoke.

Yusuf nodded. "We lit every thatched roof and stacked fires inside the buildings until we ran out of torch grass."

"I hope it works," said Ona. "Otherwise these people's homes and shops will have been destroyed for nothing."

"The Narlaw would have done worse," said Yusuf. "They would have torched the Outer Town and used the burning wood as missiles to throw over the wall. That's what happened in Altenheim."

Ona nodded. Alice and Nara had told everyone at the council about that battle. "I wish there was something more I could do," she said. "Everyone else has a purpose, a skill. I've tried to help the Whisperers, but I've mostly just been getting in their way." Frustration rose in her throat, threatening to come out as tears. She swallowed hard. A thought suddenly occurred to her. "Did someone send you to look after me?" she asked.

Yusuf frowned. "No!" he said. "I came here because I wanted to see you. I was worried—"

"You were worried," interrupted Ona, "because you know I can't look after myself. I might get kidnapped again, or blunder out on to the front lines…"

"No," said Yusuf. "You said you wanted to help, and so do I. I thought we could help together."

Ona looked up at her friend. "All of this – the war, being kidnapped – it's changed me. You saw what my life was like before. All I did was sit and drink tea and gossip with people who were only spending time with me because I was a princess. I don't want that any more, but I don't know what else to do. I don't fit in anywhere now."

Yusuf watched her, his dark eyes thoughtful. "I can't imagine what you must have gone through," he said finally. "Being kidnapped by the Narlaw. You've been braver than most of the armed soldiers in this city. It's not right that everyone's treating you like a little girl." He looked her in the eye. "I'm sorry," he said. "I'll help in any way I can. Just tell me what you want us to do. You want to fight at the front? Then we'll fight at the front. Just say it."

Ona laughed. "Now you're being silly," she said. "But thank you. There are people downstairs who need our help. We'll start there, no matter what anyone says."

Together, they marched down to the customs house kitchen, joining the other volunteers as they delivered food to those who needed it. When the food ran out they carried blankets to the people outside. Ona sweated and swept her hair from her face with grubby hands. Her legs ached, but she kept going, always with Yusuf by her side. By mid-afternoon an uneasy lull settled over the building.

It was then that the great bell on the South Gate began to toll. Ona and Yusuf hurried back to the roof, hearing more and more alarm bells ring out across the city.

Out on the southern plain the green fields had turned dark. The Narlaw army had arrived.

"There're so many of them," Yusuf muttered beside her.

Ona stared at the thousands upon thousands of demons that had emerged from the southern hills and woodlands like a slow tide. For the first time, she imagined the reality of the siege. She pictured the gates collapsing, the streets filled with demons and the people hunted down as their homes burned.

"Dawn," she whispered. "Where are you?"

Yusuf looked across at her with a question in his eyes and Ona stared back blankly. She felt the truth of what Dawn had told her deep in her bones: only the earthstone could save them now.

As dusk fell, the first fire bombs arced over the wall. The city boomed with the sound of battering rams, and the evening air flashed red with fire as the rooftops of Meridar exploded in flames.

Ona ran across the cobbled dockside towards the customs house. A tall ship blazed on the water, crackling as its timbers burned. The main mast fell with a horrifying screech, sending a vast curl of sparks out across the surface of the river. Ona covered her face against the heat as she sprinted past and darted inside, coughing as she glanced around the lobby.

"Yusuf!" she called. "I've found somewhere!"

Earlier a fire bomb had struck the clock tower at the top of the customs house and the fire was now raging out of control. They needed to evacuate.

"Yusuf!" Ona called again.

Her friend appeared at the foot of the main stairs. He held his sleeve across his face and his eyes were red and watery.

"I've found a warehouse," Ona told him. "It's not close, but it should be out of range of the fire bombs."

Yusuf nodded. "Almost everyone's at ground level," he panted. "Just a few more people on the first floor."

Ona followed him up the staircase, bounding two steps at a time.

It was difficult to breathe on the first floor. Thick smoke hovered below the ceiling and the air was sharp in Ona's throat. She stayed low and ran behind Yusuf, down a long corridor of many doors. Yusuf swung into a room at the far end. An ancient-looking man sat in the corner with his knees against his chest and a blanket over his face.

"Sir!" said Yusuf, taking a firm grip on the man's arm. "Sir, it's time to go!"

The man shrank away from him, then doubled over in a gruesome fit of coughing.

Ona ran to the man's side. "We have a safe place for you," she said. "Don't worry, we'll help you down the stairs. But I'm afraid we have to go now."

The man peered into her eyes and nodded.

Ona and Yusuf raised him from the floor by his shoulders and carried him between them, out into the corridor. By the time they reached the stairs the air was almost too hot to breathe. Ona glanced up and saw flames licking the wooden banisters of the upper floors. She trod carefully, trying not to rush as she and Yusuf helped the man down the staircase.

On the ground floor they shuffled into the hall where everyone had gathered. Hundreds of faces turned to them as they entered. The few militia who had been stationed there had been called away to fight at the River Gate. Ona and Yusuf were all these people had left.

"We have a safe place!" called Ona. "It's out of range of the Narlaw. But we have to go now."

A murmur rippled through the packed hall.

"Everyone who has the strength, help support someone who doesn't," she said. "Form a line at the door – and no rushing!"

Ona led the way and Yusuf stayed in the hall to shepherd people out.

The docks were in chaos. People charged out of the side streets, dropping buckets into the river before struggling back into the city to fight against the flames. Ona headed north at a slow, steady pace. She checked back constantly, scanning the long line of faces, right to the end where she could just make out Yusuf.

The fighting at the gates sounded awful, screams and curses mixed with the endless pounding of the battering rams. Ona wondered desperately about Alice and the other Whisperers. Palace guards raced past on horseback. A fire bomb hissed nearby and Ona ducked instinctively. It burst over the stone frontage of an old building. Sparks rained to the cobbles along with chunks of masonry and burning wood. It felt as if the whole world was coming to an end.

Eventually, they reached the northern edge of

the docklands and the empty warehouse Ona had found. She led the refugees straight inside and they dispersed, taking shelter along the walls.

Ona sank into an exhausted crouch beside the open doors. She watched the refugees file in, smiling encouragement as best she could, but her lungs stung from the smoke and her back and legs were painfully stiff.

When she saw Yusuf she rose to her feet.

"It's a good spot," he said.

Ona nodded. The streets were much quieter here and the closest fires were about two hundred paces to the south. She stepped out on to the docks and peered downriver towards the chaos of the city wall.

"How long do you think we can hold out?" she asked.

"I don't know," Yusuf replied. He opened his mouth to continue, but held back.

Ona knew the unspoken words were *not long*. She watched as a fire bomb soared into the city, trailing sparks like a comet. It was almost beautiful.

# CHAPTER 10

The western mountains shone gold and purple under a brilliant sunset. Dawn gazed at the jagged peaks and the dark forested foothills as she rode. She and Gabriel had been on the move all day, almost without rest, with Ebony and Titus soaring above them.

The birds had led them safely from the mine all the way to the foothills in the west. Ebony had already scouted as far as Meridar. She had seen an army of thousands of demons crashing against the city walls.

*They won't hold for long*, Ebony had told Dawn. *We have to hurry.*

They rode as fast as the horses would allow, winding through deep valleys, fording rivers and crossing open vales that left Dawn feeling dangerously exposed. All she wanted was to be back in Meridar with the earthstone, but she simply couldn't risk running into any more demons.

Now dusk was darkening the world and Dawn could feel her mare's weariness grow deeper by the mile. They had reached the edge of a sparse copse of white willow trees and a broad grassy plain opened out before them. A modest river curved through the plain, shining in the low light. Further west Dawn could see the deep forest that led up through steep foothills to the mountains themselves. She reined her horse in at the edge of the trees and turned back to Gabriel. "This seems like a good place to rest," she said.

"A beautiful spot," said Gabriel, smiling tiredly. He dismounted and gazed across the river plain.

Dawn climbed down from her saddle and tethered her mare to a tree. As she stretched her back and legs she watched Gabriel discreetly. He seemed to breathe the world into his lungs as he stood, calmly taking in the view.

"We can rest for a few hours," said Dawn, "get some sleep, maybe, but we can't stop for long."

"Then I'd better make the most of it," said Gabriel, dropping on to a tussock of grass and placing his hands behind his head as a pillow.

Dawn sat, unsleeping, as night fell over the river plain and the hills and mountains beyond. She held her belt pouch in her hand, feeling the weight of the necklace and its precious stones. She untied the pouch and dropped the necklace on to her lap.

Gabriel breathed loudly beside her, fast asleep.

The earthstone sat tight in its gold setting, its dark surface gleaming as Dawn rotated the necklace in the dim moonlight. She recalled the battle back at the crossroads. The power behind the stone was overwhelming and Dawn knew instinctively that it had been at the limit of her ability to keep control of the earthstone. If only she could form a circle and link with the other Whisperers. According to her diaries, Queen Amina had had almost a hundred Whisperers beside her when she banished the Narlaw a century ago. Now, there were a little over twenty Whisperers in Meridina, and it was unlikely they would all make it to Meridar.

Dawn placed the tip of her finger on the earthstone and immediately drew it away. Even half a second of contact left her breathless, exhilarated and afraid.

The branches above her head creaked and Dawn glanced up.

*You're not sleeping?* said Ebony. She dropped down from the branches and hopped to Dawn's side, glancing at Gabriel, who was lying with his mouth wide open.

*I don't think I can*, said Dawn. She slipped Ona's necklace back into her belt pouch, being careful not to touch the earthstone. *We need to get going soon anyway.*

Ebony stretched her wings, her feathers sweeping over the grass. *The demons are spreading out*, she said. *They must know you're trying to get to Meridar. I spotted another patrol of them a few miles to the east.*

*Is the city surrounded?* asked Dawn.

*Not yet*, Ebony said, *but soon the northern wall*

*will be the only way in.*

Dawn peered out into the night. *I need you to take a message to the Whisperers*, she said. *We have to let the palace know we're coming, that we've got the earthstone.*

*Of course*, said Ebony.

Dawn closed her eyes for a few moments, and waves of tiredness rolled up her spine and made her shiver. *Right*, she said, rising to her feet. She touched Gabriel's shoulder and he woke with a slurred mumble, peering up at her sleepily. "Sorry," Dawn said. "But it's time to go."

*I'll head for the palace*, said Ebony, stretching her wings in preparation.

*And you can definitely make them understand?* asked Dawn.

*I'm a raven*, said Ebony. *It's what we do.*

Dawn nodded. *Thank you*, she said, *and fly high. Don't take any risks.*

Ebony clacked her beak and let out a long caw. Then, with swift, powerful wing strokes, she rose and disappeared into the night sky. Dawn stared after her for a moment, then she saw that Gabriel was mounted and ready to go. She clambered up into the saddle. "Come on," she said to her horse. "Let's get you home to Meridar."

They rode through the night, Dawn scanning the terrain ahead, reaching into the pitch-black woodland and out across the river valleys. On her left, always, were the mountains, and beneath them the deep, deep shadows of the forested hills. Those forests were over a mile away, but Dawn still felt how they bristled with life – more than she'd felt anywhere since the Narlaw invasion had destroyed so much. A group of animals was moving north behind that wall of trees. Dawn could sense the large size of the group, but nothing more. She mentioned it to Gabriel.

"As long as they're not demons," he said with a shrug.

Dawn agreed with him, but this strange group of creatures still added to her sense of unease.

Morning crept across the sky and Dawn clutched the reins limply as her mare carried her down a shallow incline towards another low, grassy plain. As Dawn stared hard at the coming sunrise she saw a grey smear of smoke in the far distance. It could only be Meridar.

It was then that Titus swooped low over their heads with a piercing screech. Gabriel twisted in his saddle and Titus wheeled to the east, diving then rising again, and Gabriel muttered a curse under his breath. "Narlaw," he said. "There, by the hills."

At the eastern edge of the plain another, much smaller, column of smoke rose into the brightening sky.

Dawn looked at Gabriel. "Perhaps they won't see us…" she said.

"Perhaps," said Gabriel. "Titus will let us know."

Dawn nodded, nudging her horse into a trot as they set out across the plain.

The ground was marshy and their pace was slow. Dawn felt trapped between the Narlaw army in the east and the mountains in the west. She kept her senses sharp, and willed her horse to move faster, but the mare's hooves sank deep into the soft ground.

She stroked the horse's neck, whispering words of kindness and gratitude. The sun rose and the black smoke of Meridar rose with it. Dawn watched the sky and waited anxiously for Ebony's return.

It was almost noon when the demons came after them.

Titus dipped and whirled in the sky, screeching his warning to Gabriel.

"They're coming!" said Gabriel.

Dawn dug her ankles into her horse's flanks. "We have to get out of this marsh," she said. "We might be able to outrun them on solid ground, but not here."

Gabriel raced to catch up as Dawn's mare found a burst of speed, snorting at the effort, mud grasping at her every step. Ahead Dawn could see a spur of hillside that seemed to be the quickest exit from the marsh. She touched the necklace as it swung in her belt pouch – she would only use the earthstone if she had to.

"I can see them!" shouted Gabriel.

Dawn turned to see four or five dark shapes

against the green of the marsh. They were tiny, almost a mile away, but gaining fast. She looked back at the hillside they were aiming for and realized they would never make it in time. They would have to stand and fight.

Dawn reined in her panting mare and turned her to face the coming demons. She counted five of them. By their furious pace she judged she would have two minutes to prepare, maybe three.

"You can take them, right?" asked Gabriel. "You've got the earthstone."

Dawn didn't speak. She was already settling into the earth trance, one hand ready above her open belt pouch.

The demons grew closer. She could see their grey eyes now, their inhuman movements. She expanded her senses, reaching out towards the demons. It struck her then – another rushing mass of life on the marsh. She spun to face the foothills and the forest.

Low and sleek and beautiful, a pack of wolves raced into the open.

Gabriel gasped as he saw them, too, the wolves

outstripping the demons for pace across the waterlogged ground.

Dawn gripped her mare's reins as the wolves flew past. There must have been thirty, forty of them. Her horse whinnied in fear, spinning on the spot as the wolves charged at the approaching demons with a great chorus of howls. Fifty paces away the two forces collided.

Dawn held on to the earth trance, awestruck, as the demons fell under a barrage of leaping, snarling fur. Whelps and cries rose alongside the furious sounds of attack. The demons fought back and Dawn saw a wolf fly through the air, twisting frantically to right itself.

Before Dawn could recover from her shock, a silence fell on the marsh. The tangle of fur separated and the wolves stalked quickly away from the immobile forms of the demons. Several walked a short way and then fell. Several more lay still beside the bodies of the demons.

Dawn shared an incredulous look with Gabriel. Her pulse raced. The wild was fighting back.

"We should help them," Dawn said, watching the surviving wolves tend to their injured.

Gabriel nodded, still shocked, and the horses twitched nervously.

Dawn scanned the wolf pack until she saw the largest of them – white with ice-blue eyes – striding through the battleground. Dawn whispered an offer of help and the white wolf suddenly stopped, its eyes boring into her. Dawn repeated her offer.

But the big wolf bared its teeth and growled.

Dawn pulled away with her senses, realizing she had overstepped her bounds. These were wild wolves, not companions, and they didn't want her help. Dawn met the wolf's hard gaze for a moment longer then lowered her eyes. When she glanced across at Gabriel he was staring at her strangely.

"We should go," said Dawn. She nudged her mare and the horse shook her mane, hurrying gratefully towards the northern edge of the marsh.

They rode north-east over a patch of golden-brown heath, winding between prickly gorse bushes and isolated stretches of marsh. The afternoon wore on and Dawn watched the skies for Ebony's return. As they forded a shallow river Dawn felt her companion's presence again. She stared into the bank of white cloud that had settled over them and saw a black dot growing gradually larger.

*Here!* she called.

Ebony swept through the sky then dived, flapping wildly to slow down for her landing.

Dawn flinched as Ebony's huge wings batted the air around her head.

*The wall's been breached*, said Ebony, as she adjusted her grip on Dawn's shoulder. *They're holding on, but only just.*

*How long do we have?* asked Dawn.

*I don't know*, said Ebony. *The Whisperers are spread all over the city, wherever the fighting's fiercest. They might hold on for another day, but ... it doesn't look good.*

Dawn noticed Gabriel watching them expectantly.

*Is Princess Ona all right?* asked Dawn.

*I couldn't find her*, said Ebony. *She's out in the city*

*somewhere. But I gave your message to Mika. She's at the palace. She whispered to me, said she'd wait for you there.*

Dawn looked over at Gabriel. "The city's falling," she said. "We have to move fast."

Gabriel peered across the heath, directly east towards Meridar then up at Titus, gliding overhead. "If we ride hard we can be there by nightfall," he said.

*Are you ready to fly?* Dawn asked Ebony.

*I think so*, her companion replied, stretching her wings.

*Then lead us to Meridar*, said Dawn.

# CHAPTER 11

The ceiling of the warehouse shuddered and boomed. Ona glanced up and saw the wooden crossbeams crack. Dust and plaster fell like rain. "Move!" she cried, waving the few remaining refugees over to the far side of the warehouse.

The cries of battle sounded from just a few streets away. The Stonecutter's Gate had fallen that morning and the front lines had slowly crept north towards the warehouse. It was only a matter of time before Ona, Yusuf and the refugees would be caught in the battle.

"The cart's ready!"

Ona turned to see Yusuf at the warehouse doors. All day he had been ferrying people to the relative safety of the palace while Ona stayed at the warehouse. Only a small fraction of the refugees remained now.

"The next twenty," Ona called, "come with me!"

The gathered people shifted and muttered among themselves. Ona pointed to the chosen ones. She tried to reassure them as they stumbled out.

Another direct hit shook the warehouse.

"Keep going!" said Ona. "It's all right! Just keep going!"

She glanced up and saw flames in the roof beams. "We need to hurry," she whispered to Yusuf as he ushered them towards the cart.

"I know," he said. "I'll be back as soon as I can."

Ona squeezed his arm before he climbed up. The horses jerked into motion and the cart clattered away over the cobbles.

Back inside, Ona counted the remaining refugees. It would take one or two more journeys to get them all to safety. She looked at their tired, grime-streaked faces and saw fear, defiance, anxiety, resignation. Ona forced her own fear and exhaustion aside and realized that she was finally fulfilling a purpose.

She allowed herself a brief, grim smile. Then another fire bomb crashed against the warehouse roof and she ducked, covering her face as dust and sparks cascaded through the air around her.

Ona was at the warehouse door waiting anxiously for Yusuf's return when a lone rider galloped over the quayside.

It was a palace guard, her black plaited hair streaming behind her as she rode. "Retreat to the palace!" she cried. "The West Gate has fallen!" Her bugle rang out mournfully over the docks as she vanished into the smoke, heading for the battle lines.

"We have to go!" said Ona, running back inside.

Eight scared faces stared back at her – the last of the refugees.

"The West Gate has fallen," said Ona. "If we don't move now, we'll be cut off from the palace."

She didn't have to explain any further. There was a broad avenue that led from the West Gate to Founder's Square in the centre of the city. If the demons had broken through in the west, there was little to stop them charging down that avenue and trapping everyone in the south-west of the city between the two battle fronts.

The refugees gathered around the princess. With them were two militia volunteers – a young woman armed with a short sword and an elderly man with a rusty old spear. Both had been cut off from their units and had taken shelter with Ona.

"I grew up in these streets," said the man, squinting at Ona through bloodshot eyes. "We can take the smuggler's alleys to the Fiveways – maybe cut north from there?"

"Good," said Ona. The Fiveways was a junction on the western avenue, but apart from that she knew nothing of the dense warren of streets around the docks. "Can you lead the way?" she asked him.

The man bowed awkwardly. "I can, Your Highness."

"Then let's go," said Ona.

They left the warehouse in single file, the militia man taking the lead, leaning on his spear as if it were a walking staff.

Ona slipped into the group near the rear, alongside the young militia woman, and together they kept watch over the rest of the refugees.

They weaved left, then right, then left again, and the militia man stopped up ahead. Ona peered past him and saw a patch of sky between the tightly packed buildings. A bugle call echoed, again and again. She couldn't tell if it was coming from the south or the west. The militia man raised his arm, beckoning her to join him, and Ona squeezed down the narrow alleyway.

"Fiveways," the man said.

Ona peered out on to a broad junction, its grey flagstones littered with masonry and burning timber. The grand buildings around the junction's edge were pocked with craters and streaked with ash. For a moment nothing moved, then a riderless horse charged past.

"There's more coming," muttered the militia man and in the distance, Ona saw more horses emerge from a thick wall of smoke, some with riders and some without. There were people running beside them, too. Ona squinted. "The retreating forces," she said.

"We should cross now," said the man. "Once the army gets here it'll be chaos."

Ona couldn't tear her gaze from the coming mass of soldiers. There were more and more of them spilling out of the smoke, filling the broad avenue as they charged. Something wasn't right. The way they moved. The sheer speed of the foot soldiers...

"No," Ona muttered. "No, no, no."

She glanced across at the wide stretch of open road, then back at the bedraggled refugees lined up anxiously behind her, sharing a worried glance with the militia woman at the back of the line.

"We won't make it," said Ona.

"What do you mean?" asked the militia man.

"Look at them," she hissed. "They're not our soldiers. They're Narlaw!"

The man's eyes widened. He cursed and lifted his spear.

"No!" said Ona, dragging him back into the

shadow of the alleyway. "Everybody back," she ordered, and the group shuffled deeper into the alley. "Round there!" she hissed, pointing to a corner that led away into the depths of the neighbourhood.

Ona glanced back once before turning the corner. She saw men and women fly past at inhuman speed. Hooves thundered and the riders sat rigid on their mounts. Ona pressed herself against the wall of the alley, breathing hard. The demons must have smashed through the city's western defences. They had a free run all the way to the centre – maybe even to the palace.

Ona squeezed her eyes shut, wishing she was somewhere else, wishing that the Narlaw had never come to Meridina and that none of this had ever happened. But when she opened them she was still there in the alleyway, listening to the furious advance of the demons. If it hadn't been for the scared, expectant faces of the refugees she would have curled up on the ground and wept.

"We have to keep moving," she said. "We have to try to reach the palace."

The young militia woman stepped up from the back of the line. "There're soldiers nearby," she said, pointing to the south. "The retreat's about to reach us."

Ona nodded. "Right," she said, "so we can join up with them. That'll give us a better chance." Ona forced herself to focus, to think.

"Sir," she said, addressing the elderly militia man. "Would you guide us to the retreating soldiers? We have to stay off the main streets."

"Aye," said the man, gripping his spear with both hands.

"I'll watch the rear," the young woman said, drawing the short sword from her belt.

They set off down the alleyway past empty houses, fires crackling overhead. Straws of smouldering thatch floated down around them as they coughed their way through clouds of smoke.

Ona listened to the battle noise as they approached the front line. Ahead, the militia man reached a junction where the alley met a cobbled street. Then the battle came to them.

A woman charged past the junction in the blue cloak of a palace guard with several green-clad militia following, blood on their faces and panic in their eyes. The palace guard glanced into the alley and saw Ona and her refugees. She gawped for half a second as more soldiers arrived. She spun suddenly. "Get down!" she screamed.

A blinding ball of flame shot along the cobbled street at head height. The soldiers dropped to the floor with their hands over their heads. In the alley, Ona threw herself against the wall as a fire bomb exploded into burning splinters right across the junction.

The guard jumped to her feet and waved the soldiers into the alley with her sword. "Go!" she shouted.

They scrambled past the refugees as another fire bomb ripped down the adjoining street, exploding somewhere out of view.

"What are you doing here?" the guard asked, staring from face to face.

Ona stepped forwards. "We were on our way

to the palace," she said. "There are demons on the western avenue. We were cut off."

The guard cursed loudly. "That's bad news. They've broken through the southern lines and scattered everyone. They're pushing us west towards the docks. We were hoping to go north, but … well." She glared up the alleyway past Ona and the refugees, as if she could bore a hole in the Narlaw lines with pure hatred.

Another fire bomb flew past the junction. It went high, crashing into the eaves of a building and sending flames and masonry tumbling to the ground. Ona watched the corner of the alley where two soldiers crouched, aiming longbows down the street towards the source of the fire bombs. They let loose and reloaded, aiming carefully, but their quivers were almost empty of arrows.

"Report!" the guard shouted.

One of the archers peeled away and ran to the guard's side. "Less than fifty paces away," the man said, "but I can see militia in the side streets – Valderin's group, maybe."

"If Valderin's holding fast then we are, too," said the guard. She wiped sweat from her face with her sword hand. Ona noticed that her other arm was injured. It looked bad.

Suddenly Ona felt an arrow whisk past, then another. Then she was barged aside, falling into the terrified refugees as the guard sergeant charged past. A pair of demons were advancing from the other end of the alley.

The first of the Narlaw – a huge man – swung its fists at the palace guard even as her sword thrust deep into its chest. The guard fell to the ground.

More arrows flew.

Ona saw the second demon – a tall girl in a patterned dress – rise from the ground. At its feet lay the young militia woman. Nearby the guard sergeant rolled and growled under the weight of the man-demon. The demon raised two hands above its head, ready to bring them down on the defenceless guard.

Ona turned away. She couldn't bear to watch.

Then a high-pitched snarl grabbed her attention. She saw the guard back on her feet, gripping her sword. There was a flash of golden-yellow and a black-tipped tail. Another snarl ripped through the air and Ona saw Flame the leopard pin the man-demon to the ground. More arrows flew and the girl-demon fell with a horrible cry.

At the far end of the alley two crouching figures emerged. For a moment they were as still as stone. The man-demon wailed and thrashed under the huge paws of the leopard, then its wail was cut short. Both demons were suddenly gone.

Nara and Tuanne strode down the alley, Tuanne's red-striped monkey on her shoulder.

"This way," Nara called to the stunned guards and refugees. She caught sight of Ona and smiled. Flame trotted to her side, breathing hard and flicking her tail.

The group wound through empty streets. Tuanne led the way, pausing and listening, scanning for demons. She led them through a tiny door and into a long room that could have been a kind of banquet hall. Light streaked in through several holes in the ceiling and the far wall was piled high with a barricade of furniture and fallen timber. Injured soldiers lay everywhere and at the end of the hall, near the rumbling barricade, Ona saw Valderin, the captain of the palace guard. And beside him stood Alice, one hand resting on Storm's proud grey-black shoulders.

# CHAPTER 12

Dawn and Gabriel rode their horses hard across the rising heathlands north of Meridar. A flickering orange glow surrounded the southern half of the city and, as Dawn watched Meridar burn, Ebony materialized from the evening sky.

*The gates are blocked*, said Ebony, flapping down on to the pommel of Dawn's saddle. *The West Gate is down and half the city is swarming with demons.*

*Then we need another way in*, said Dawn, an idea already forming in her mind.

Gabriel rode up beside them, his grey mare panting hard as she heaved him up the last section of sloping heath. "Bad news, by any chance?" he asked with a wry smile.

"We can't use the city gates," said Dawn, "but I

think I can get us into the palace."

Ebony cocked her head and gave Dawn a quizzical look. *As far as I know*, she said, *you haven't learned to fly.*

Dawn shook her head and smiled. "The aqueduct," she said.

Ebony cawed in realization.

Gabriel frowned. "The what?"

"It carries water from the hills straight into the palace. It was broken when I left, but we might still be able to get across." She turned to Ebony. *Can you take a look?* she asked. *See if the demons have found it yet, and if the collapsed section was ever repaired.*

*On my way*, said Ebony, rising from the saddle and sweeping away, low over the golden heath.

Ebony's scouting mission didn't take long.

*It's heavily guarded*, she said on her return. *No demons, just Guards of the Sun. The gap has been repaired and they've got a ladder for the palace walls.*

*Good*, said Dawn. *That's our way in.*

164

As they neared the city, the sound of battle floated on the wind like a coming thunderstorm. Ebony rode with Dawn on the front of the saddle, bobbing her head in time with the mare's tired shoulders. She was tired, too. She had flown more miles in the last few days than she had in all her years in Meridar put together.

*What on earth is that?* Ebony whispered suddenly. She spun on the saddle and flapped into the air, facing back up the hill.

Dawn twisted in the saddle. The sky was a deep blue, almost black. She saw the outline of Gabriel as he rode a few paces behind them. *What is it?* Dawn asked. *I can't sense any demons.*

*Not demons*, said Ebony. *Ravens.*

They swooped down the hillside, black shadows turning and wheeling, filling the sky. The air was wild with caws as the ravens formed a vast circle over the heads of the riders. Dawn stared up in astonishment. She sensed her companion, lost in the storm of wings.

*They've come to help us*, cried Ebony.

*Just like the wolves*, said Dawn.

They reached the aqueduct as night fell. Torchlight flickered, reflected in the smooth liquid surface of the waterway. Dawn saw the gold and red uniforms of the Guard of the Sun.

"Halt!" shouted one of them. "State your name and purpose!"

Dawn guided her horse a few short steps on to the aqueduct. The water ran like silver in the moonlight.

"I'm Dawn, the Palace Whisperer!" she called back. She counted eight guards on the aqueduct and saw the silhouettes of many more above them on the battlements.

The guards conferred among themselves and a message was shouted up the ladder to the battlements.

Dawn sat with growing impatience until, a moment later, a familiarly shrill voice called down. "You've returned too late, Whisperer!"

*Lady Tremaine*, said Ebony. *This wasn't the welcoming party I was hoping for.*

"We have the earthstone!" Dawn shouted, swinging down from the saddle and splashing into the shallow waters. "Tell your guards to take care of our horses. We're coming up!"

The ravens circled and swooped as Dawn and Gabriel strode across the aqueduct and climbed the swaying rope ladder into the Palace of the Sun. The guards watched the whirling mass of birds uncomfortably, ducking as the huge shadows swept around their heads.

Lady Tremaine stood a few paces away, staring at Dawn with a glare that was more uncertain than usual, more afraid. "So you have the stone," she said. "King Eneron will be interested to see—"

"I've got no time for the king," Dawn interrupted, hurrying down the stairs that clung to the inside of the high palace wall and leaving the warden behind her in stunned silence. Now she had finally returned to Meridar she felt urgency boiling through her more intensely than ever. She concentrated on the narrow stairs, the same stairs she had climbed with Captain Valderin after the first Narlaw spy had sabotaged the aqueduct. It seemed like such a long time ago now, but Dawn's feeling of vertigo was the same. Ebony flapped above her, waiting until Dawn had reached the base of the stairs before landing on her shoulder.

*Where was Mika last time you saw her?* Dawn asked.

*In the Spiral Tower*, Ebony replied.

*Good*, said Dawn. *We can work there.*

She swerved through dank corridors with Gabriel close behind, running up stairs and shoving doors until they emerged into the dim light of one of the lesser-used palace courtyards. The boom of battle thrummed the air. A servant boy sprinted across the courtyard carrying a basket and Dawn watched him run towards a doorway. Hungry faces peered out. Refugees. Dawn reached the base of the Spiral Tower. The desire to fight back against the Narlaw was like a fever in her blood.

"So this is where you live?" asked Gabriel. "Nice."

He scanned the sky for Titus, and Dawn peered up at the ornate curves of the tower's summit.

The ravens flocked there in their hundreds.

*I'll fly up and see if Mika's there*, said Ebony.

*Thank you*, whispered Dawn. She turned to Gabriel as she started into the tower. "I hope you like stairs," she said.

Dawn climbed the curved, echoing stairway with Gabriel close behind. The noise of war rumbled constantly in the background, crashing in whenever they passed a window. The familiarity of the climb was made sad and strange by the battle outside.

*Mika's not here*, said Ebony. She flapped in through an un-shuttered window and perched on the ledge. *She must be defending the palace walls. I'll try to find her and send her to you.*

Dawn nodded. So the palace itself was under siege now? She laboured up the final set of stairs and found herself on the curving corridor that led to her chambers. The door was unlocked. She pushed it open and stepped inside.

Everything was as she'd left it – maps of Meridar and the surrounding country spread open on the huge desk; stacks of books beside each seat; the doors to the balcony wide open. She passed through the main chamber, thinking of the events and the people that had taken her so far away and brought her back again. She thought of Loren. She thought of Ona and Valderin and Valderin's guards who had died to save the princess. Then she stepped on to the balcony and the blazing, thundering city unfurled before her. The south-west quarter was nothing but fire. Flaming missiles arced and the fires of the demon army stretched out on to the plain. Below, at the palace walls, the huge defensive gates boomed and creaked under the weight of the attack. The walls were lined with archers. She searched for Mika, or any other Whisperers, but the tiny figures were camouflaged by night and veiled by the drifting smoke.

"I don't know how they survived this long," Dawn said.

Gabriel arrived by her side, leaning over the parapet, his blue eyes awed by the scale of the destruction. "But they're still fighting," he said, pointing out into the city.

He was right. There were pockets of resistance around the East Gate, in the docklands and the central square. Dawn's heart surged with pride and with the desire to win this war once and for all. She touched her belt pouch and felt the weight of the necklace within.

"It ends tonight," she said.

# CHAPTER 13

Dawn stood on the balcony with her eyes clenched shut and her senses dizzied by the surging Narlaw army.

*I can't find them*, she whispered in frustration. *They're too far away. How am I going to form a circle if I can't even find the other Whisperers?*

*Keep trying*, said Ebony. Her claws scratched against the carved stone parapet as she shuffled to and fro. *They must be down there somewhere.*

*Unless they're not*, said Dawn. *Unless they're already in the ghost-sleep. Or worse. I can't banish the whole demon army alone. Not even with the earthstone. It's impossible.*

The parade ground below was manic with activity. Missiles flew and crashed on to the flagstones of the yard, showering fire and masonry. The high outer walls were lined with soldiers – palace guards, militia volunteers and Guards of the Sun. In the streets beyond, Dawn saw the demons thronging. Their numbers seemed inexhaustible.

Ebony turned to face the chambers behind them. *Mika*, she said to Dawn.

A moment later footsteps pattered in the outer corridor and the door swung open. There was Mika, in her embroidered coat, breathing hard and staring with a wild kind of hope at Dawn. "You made it!" she gasped, rushing across the room towards her. Mika's arctic fox companion, Star, waited crouching in the doorway along with Zabeh, the young soldier.

Dawn smiled. Her first meeting with Mika and Star had been like a blessing from the earth. They had appeared, seemingly from nowhere, while Dawn had sat cradling the injured Captain Valderin and despairing over Princess Ona, who lay unconscious. Mika had raised the princess from the ghost-sleep and saved the life of Captain Valderin, escorting him back to Meridar under her care.

"It's so good to see you, Mika," said Dawn, grasping her in a tight embrace. "I wish I could find the others, too."

Mika nodded as they drew apart, blushing slightly. "There were sixteen of us before the fighting started," she said. "I don't know how many are left, but when I was down on the palace walls, every now and then I felt a Whisperer's presence. They're doing their best to get back here. I know it."

"They won't get through now," said Dawn. "We'll have to form a circle some other way. I thought we could link from a distance, but I can't seem to make contact with anyone from up here." She looked to Mika for help.

"I've never linked before," said Mika. "Nara said that she and Tuanne linked with each other from a hundred paces away. But it might not be possible with everyone spread out across the city."

Dawn felt desperation creep into her thoughts. She glanced at Ebony, who was watching her closely. *I don't think we can do it*, said Dawn. *Not from here. We're too far from the others.*

*You don't know that*, Ebony replied.

Dawn was aware that everyone was watching her, awaiting her response. She knew from Queen Amina's diaries that the circle had been formed with Amina at its centre, her links with the other Whisperers branching out like the spokes of a cartwheel. Dawn sighed, her hand moving unconsciously to her belt pouch and the solid weight of the necklace. If only the others had made it to the palace. They could have stood together, all of the Whisperers hand in hand like sisters, protected by the palace walls.

"We have to leave," Dawn muttered. "We have to leave the palace."

*What?* asked Ebony. *Have you seen what's going on out there?*

"If the Whisperers can't come to us," said Dawn, "then we have to go to them. We need to be at the centre for the circle to work."

"But the palace is under siege!" argued Zabeh. "The whole Narlaw army is hammering at the gates. Are we supposed to just stroll through all those demons?"

"There must be a way," said Dawn. "There has to be." She paused, unsure if what she was saying was true, but at the same time she was filled with a powerful feeling of pride and conviction. "Look at us," she said. "Look how far we've all come." She swept her gaze around the room, taking in Ebony, Mika and Star, Gabriel, Titus and Zabeh. "We can do it – this one last thing. I know we can."

*It's too dangerous*, urged Ebony. *You can't go out there. It's a mad thing to do. You'll be killed or captured before you get anywhere... You—*

*It's the only way*, Dawn interrupted. *You have to trust me now, Ebony. Please.*

Ebony tilted her head, folding and unfolding her wings nervously. She shuffled along the parapet and stared out into the flame-lit sky.

Silence filled the chamber and Dawn felt more exhausted than she ever had before.

It was Gabriel who spoke eventually.

"I can send Titus out," he said. "Perhaps he could find the other Whisperers? He could come back and then lead us to them?"

Dawn's heart surged with gratitude. "That's good," she said. "That could work." She looked across at Ebony. *We need to find them quickly*, she said. *Can you and Titus do it?*

*We can try*, said Ebony. *But with just the two of us, and the battle going on…*

*Wait!* said Dawn, as an idea burst upon her. "The ravens!" she said aloud. "The ravens can help us, too!"

Ebony cawed loudly. *Of course!* she said.

*Can you talk to them?* Dawn asked. *Ask them to send a message to all the Whisperers they can find. The Whisperers need to break away from the fighting however they can. Stay safe and wait for me to link with them. Tell them I'm coming!*

Ebony cawed and flapped into the air, Titus swooping out behind her.

Dawn turned to Mika, Zabeh and Gabriel. "We have to get out of the palace," she said. "We have to find a way through, so that I can be surrounded by all the other Whisperers."

Star came forwards, nuzzling into Mika's legs,

and Dawn saw immediately that the two were whispering.

A few moments later Mika looked up urgently. "Star knows a way out," she said.

It seemed to take forever to reach the edge of the palace. They had followed Star, running along behind the little white fox through corridors, stairways and courtyards, weaving through rooms that Dawn had never set foot in before. Finally, they came to a storehouse, three floors high, that was attached to the western section of the palace wall.

"This way," said Mika, translating Star's instructions for the others.

They darted inside the storehouse and began climbing a set of bare stone stairs lit by wall-mounted torches.

As she climbed, Dawn called to Ebony. *We'll be out of the palace soon*, she said. *We need to know where the Whisperers are.*

*The ravens are spreading out*, Ebony replied after

a short pause. *They'll find the Whisperers and pass your message on. As soon as they've done that I'll know where to send you.*

As she climbed the stairs Dawn felt the familiar emotions of flight through the bond – focus, exhilaration, physical strain. She could tell her companion was flying low and fast.

*I think Titus has found something*, Ebony said at last. *Some dense fighting near the docklands... Wait... Yes, the ravens are flocking there, too... I'm going in.*

*Be careful!* said Dawn. *And tell me what you see.* She reached the top of the stairs and almost ran into the back of Gabriel. In front of him, in a small dark storeroom, Mika was leaning out of the room's only window.

"It's a tough climb, but it's possible," said Zabeh as Dawn and Gabriel entered.

Dawn reached the window and leaned out. Star was perched triumphantly on top of the palace wall, some six paces away from the window. The night sky flickered behind her with the yellow-gold of nearby flames.

"The window ledge extends that way," Mika said, turning to Dawn. "Then it's a leap from there on to that buttress."

Dawn studied the gap. It wasn't impossible, but the three-storey drop to the courtyard made her stomach contract.

"Star says the way down is easier," said Mika. "And the streets are quiet there. It's a dead-end alley and the entrance isn't visible from the main street."

Dawn nodded, peering up at Star. "She's a clever one," she said.

Mika beamed at the compliment.

"Right then," said Dawn. "Who wants to go first?"

Zabeh climbed out on to the window ledge and shuffled along to the end, the toes of her boots overhanging the ledge. Then she leaped, with cat-like agility, on to the wide buttress that jutted from the palace wall.

On the ledge, the wind was more powerful than Dawn had expected and she pressed herself against the wall of the storehouse with all her weight. A fire bomb boomed somewhere nearby and Dawn thought she felt the building wobble behind her.

"It's all right," called Zabeh. "No worse than hopping over a stream."

*Except for the deadly drop down to the flagstones*, thought Dawn. She took a deep breath and shifted her boots slowly along the ledge, all the way to the end. The gap loomed ahead of her, but Zabeh was right. The buttress was only a pace and a half away. She angled her body, ready to jump.

*Dawn!* Ebony cried out suddenly.

Dawn swayed and gripped the brickwork behind her, terror shooting through her as she fought to keep her balance. *Not now*, she whispered back. *I'm very busy!*

*But we've found them*, said Ebony. *Alice and Nara! They're right in the centre of all the fighting. Captain Valderin's with them and so is the princess.*

*Ona?* said Dawn. *What is she doing in the middle of the danger?*

*I don't know, but I can lead you there – help you dodge the worst of the fighting.*

*Good*, said Dawn, sickness rising in her throat

as she glanced down at the courtyard far below. *Yes, just give us a moment, please.* She squeezed her eyes shut and focused. Then she looked across to the buttress and up at Star and Zabeh, waiting for her on the top of the wall.

Dawn jumped and her boots landed, solid and sure, on the stone buttress. She clambered, heart racing, up to the wall.

"See," said Zabeh. "Easy."

"Easy," repeated Dawn, her pulse thumping in her ears.

Once Mika and Gabriel had made the leap, Star led them along the wall and down into an alleyway that was more like a scrapyard. Masses of old timber leaned against the walls, along with tall stacks of barrels and crates. Star picked her way down nimbly, glancing back as the others followed slowly.

The end of the alley was blocked by a huge makeshift shop front. Star led them to a tiny gap in the structure and Dawn peered though at the empty street beyond.

*We're ready,* she called to Ebony. *Take us where*

*we need to go.*

She felt Ebony's presence racing through the night sky. Moments later, her companion was circling above the deserted street.

*You have to be careful*, said Ebony, *and do exactly what I say. There are demons everywhere.*

*We'll be careful*, said Dawn. *I promise.*

Even though she guided them through the very quietest backstreets and buildings, the little group were forced to stop and hide alarmingly often. In half an hour they had made barely a mile's progress across the city.

"There must be a quicker way," Dawn muttered to Mika as the five of them huddled near the rear of an abandoned inn. A group of ten or twelve Narlaw advanced down the cobbled lane outside.

Mika glanced across at her, wanting to speak but holding back. Dawn nodded in encouragement and finally Mika said what was on her mind.

"There's something I need to tell you," she said.

"The technique I discovered for ending the ghost-sleep. Do you remember I told you how it banished the demon involved permanently – beyond the Darklands even?"

"I remember," said Dawn.

"When I was fighting," said Mika, "on the palace walls, I found a way to do the same thing during banishment. A way to send the demons away forever."

Dawn stared at her, keenly aware of the group of demons outside the inn. "Show me," she asked Mika.

A tiny, blushing smile spread across Mika's face.

"I'll follow your lead," said Dawn. "Do you know how to link?"

"Yes," said Mika. "I think so."

Together they crept towards the front of the inn. Dawn felt Mika's presence reach out to her. She reached back and a tide of warmth spread through her body and mind.

*Ready?* asked Mika, silently now they could Whisper together.

*Ready*, said Dawn.

Mika gathered their combined strength and launched it at the demons outside.

Dawn felt herself driven deep into the substance of the Narlaw as they were caught by surprise. She felt the threads that made their shape-shifting bodies so strong. And she felt Mika rip away at them, tearing with a ferocity that seemed at odds with her timid nature.

In seconds the demons were gone.

"They're really gone," she said. "Further than the Darklands?"

"Further than anywhere," said Mika. She met Dawn's gaze with a sombre, determined look. "Next time, you try."

# CHAPTER 14

Ona stumbled and coughed as plaster dust rained down on her. The staircase swayed beneath her feet and the man she was helping to carry moaned in pain.

"Are you all right, Your Highness?" called the young medic carrying the man's shoulders, his voice floating strangely through the dust-swirled air.

"Yes," called Ona, although her voice was hoarse and her legs were about ready to collapse. "I'm fine. Let's get him upstairs."

The upper floors were still intact and, so far, the fires that raged through the neighbourhood hadn't taken hold of the building's roof. It was an old guard barracks, one that Valderin and his palace guards had fallen back to and then fortified. Alice, Nara and Tuanne were on the ground floor alongside their companions, banishing the demons that crashed against the barricaded doors. But the barricades were crumbling under the demon onslaught.

Together, Ona and the medic emerged on to the first floor. She struggled the final few steps and lay the injured man on to a pitiful bed of sacking by the wall. There were only three proper beds in the rectangular room and they had been filled long ago. Ona took the chance to rest, leaning on the window ledge. In the courtyard below she saw demons darting through the shadows. She hoped, for the thousandth time, that Yusuf was behind the palace walls and hadn't been caught up in the fighting like she had.

"Just one more," said the medic, interrupting Ona's thoughts.

She turned, trying not to let her exhaustion show, and followed the medic back down the stairs.

Alice stood with Storm, absorbed in concentration as she fought against the demons with her mind. Nara and Tuanne stood a few paces back, their companions, leopard and monkey, twining together at their feet. Valderin and his guards worked frantically to repair the barricades.

A final injured soldier needed carrying upstairs. Ona let the medic go first again, hefting the woman's ankles and stepping up on to the creaking wooden stairs. As they reached the halfway point Ona heard Alice cry out. She glanced down into the hall and saw Alice stumble back, holding her head in her hands.

"Form a line!" yelled Valderin and his guards leaped to obey him, raising their swords and facing the heaving, tumbling barricade in a ragged line.

The doors cracked and a massive splinter of wood came flying into the hall.

"Come on!" urged the medic.

Ona forced her legs to move faster. She looked back once more before she reached the hatch to the first floor. A gap had been punched through the barricade and arms reached in, grasping wildly. Ona clenched her teeth as she hefted the woman through the hatch.

A battle cry flew up the stairs – Valderin. An instant later it was joined by others, then by the ferocious cries of wolf and leopard. Timber ripped and thudded.

The barricade had fallen.

The demons had broken through.

Ona crouched beside the window, staring at the hatch. The bunk room was silent – no moaning from the injured soldiers, no talk. It seemed as if no one even dared to breathe.

Downstairs the battle was raging.

Ona stared and stared at the hatch. That was where the demons would come. Her body had turned numb. She could feel the end approaching. All they could do was wait for the demons to break through and come for them.

But downstairs, the defenders fought on. Wild noises tore through the air. She had seen Storm and Flame at work before and she willed them to fight back. She willed Nara, Tuanne and Alice to keep going, to keep banishing the demons to the Darklands. She willed Valderin to stand strong with his palace guards.

The young medic had torn an old door from the back of the bunk room and together he and Ona had laid it across the hatch. Ona caught the young man's eye. Then she realized he was staring past her, over her head to the open window.

Ona twisted and looked up. A large black bird peered down at her.

A raven.

For an instant she thought it was Ebony. Then Ona remembered something she had learned once – from Dawn or Esther … or from a book perhaps? – that ravens were messengers, that they carried the commands of the Palace Whisperer.

"Dawn," she whispered. Dawn was trying to communicate. Ona stared into the raven's deep, enquiring eyes.

The hatch thumped behind her and Ona spun in fear.

"It's me!" called Alice. "Open up!"

Ona and the medic glanced at each other then dragged the old door away from the hatch.

Alice peered up at them. "The raven," she said, breathlessly.

Ona turned and stared at the bird as the battle raged below, cries and snarls and crashing.

"Dawn's coming," said Alice. "Mika, too. They have the earthstone!"

Ona was too stunned to speak. She felt a smile spread across her face and saw a new glint of hope in Alice's eyes as she ducked away to rejoin the fight.

Ona and the medic heaved the door back across the hatch. By the time they'd done so, the raven was gone.

*Alice, Nara, Tuanne.*

Dawn reached out with her senses – out of the warehouse, past the crashing hordes of Narlaw and into the chaos of the barracks. There were so many demons. They threw themselves at the barracks doors, vanishing in groups as the Whisperers inside fought to banish them. But more demons always came.

*Can you hear me?* Dawn called inside.

*Dawn?* asked Nara.

*I'm outside*, Dawn said urgently. *Mika's with me and I have the earthstone. Can you help us get inside? Can you clear the way? Just for a moment?*

*I don't know*, said Nara. *Maybe. Just stay where you are.*

Ebony was circling above. She had steered them along the safest route she could find and they had arrived here, at the central point amid the scattered, fighting Whisperers.

*Can't you form the circle from here?* Ebony had asked when they'd first arrived at the warehouse.

But Dawn knew the circle would be so much stronger if she could stand side by side with the Whisperers inside the barracks. She knew she would only get one chance to attempt the banishment and it had to be done properly.

*Something's happening down there*, Ebony called. *Valderin's guards are advancing, pushing their way outside. The companions, too. I can see the wolf and leopard.*

Dawn jumped to her feet. *This could be it!* she said.

"What is it?" Mika asked.

"They're pushing the demons back," said Dawn. "I don't know how, but we have to be ready." She glanced down the line of faces and receieved a grim nod from Zabeh. Gabriel stood, craning to see out into the street before offering Dawn a worried but reassuring smile. Dawn turned to the half-open warehouse doors, reaching out with her senses, all the way into the barracks.

*Dawn?* called Nara, her voice wavering under the strain of the fight.

*We're here!* said Dawn. *We're ready!*

The fighting outside became even more intense. Demons kept throwing themselves at the slowly advancing guards and companions.

*What's happening, Ebony?* Dawn called out.

But before Ebony could reply, Nara's voice rang out in Dawn's head. *Now!*

"Come on!" Dawn cried, charging out into the street and glancing back briefly to make sure Mika, Gabriel and Zabeh were following her.

The demons turned and glared. For an instant Dawn froze in fear.

*Nara?* she called. *Nara! We're out here. What's…?*

Then the street outside the barracks surged with power as the Whisperers within linked together and attacked with every last scrap of strength they had. A corridor of space opened through the mass of demons and grey ash littered the ground.

Dawn sprinted into the space with the others following close behind. The surviving Narlaw stood stunned as Dawn clambered through the fallen barricade, counting her friends in behind her. Gabriel climbed through last and placed a hand on Dawn's shoulder as he passed. The palace guards began repairing the barricade immediately. Storm and Flame leaped back inside, panting hard.

"You made it!" breathed Nara as Dawn and Mika approached the other three Whisperers.

Dawn hugged each of them in turn. "Thank you,"

she said. "For getting us inside. Is there somewhere we can go? Can the guards hold the demons off for us?"

Alice and Nara shared doubtful looks and Tuanne stared at her boots.

"Upstairs," said Alice finally. "We can block ourselves in, but the defence won't last long. The demons just keep coming."

"Upstairs then," Dawn said to Gabriel, Zabeh and the gathered Whisperers. As they started up the stairs she approached Valderin.

"Don't worry," he said. "We'll take care of things here. But if you can work fast up there, we'd appreciate it." He smiled and Dawn was overwhelmed with gratitude.

The barricade boomed, then began to crackle ominously. Thin strands of smoke pushed through into the barracks. The demons were back.

Dawn hurried for the stairs, past the nervous palace guards, past Flame and Storm. As she climbed, the pounding at the barricade became frantic, wood splintering under the Narlaw assault.

She emerged through the hatch and Ona stood before her.

"It's so good to see you," said the princess, squeezing her tightly.

Dawn hugged her back. "I'm so glad you're all right," she said.

Dawn looked round to see a room full of injured guards and refugees. Everybody's eyes were on her, awaiting her command.

"It's time to end this war," she said, freeing her belt pouch and carefully removing the necklace. "We have to join together," she said to the Whisperers, "form a circle with all the other Whisperers in the city. Whatever we hear from down below, we have to keep going."

Ebony soared through the open window and landed heavily on Dawn's shoulder.

*More demons are coming*, she said. *I think word has spread. They know what you're trying to do.*

Dawn supressed a shudder of fear. She thought of Valderin and his guards, of Storm and Flame. *Then we'll have to work fast*, she said.

"Reinforce that hatch with anything you can," she said to Gabriel, Ona and Zabeh. "Whisperers, to me."

She kneeled on the floorboards near the window and waited for Mika, Nara, Tuanne and Alice to kneel around her. Dawn closed her eyes, gripping the necklace, but not yet touching the earthstone. Now was the time. Dawn's stomach fluttered with nerves as she slowly, carefully descended into the earth trance.

Ona listened anxiously as the battle became more and more desperate downstairs. She knew Valderin and his guards couldn't keep the Narlaw out for long, even with Storm and Flame fighting beside them.

Then the stack of furniture covering the hatch boomed and shook. The demons had reached the top of the stairs.

"We have to do something!" Ona shouted, swallowing her fear and panic. She flung all her weight against the barricade, grunting as the stack of beds jumped and rattled beneath her. The young medic ran over and joined her. So did Zabeh and Dawn's friend – the boy with the eagle. Below the hatch Ona heard snarling that she thought was Storm.

"It's not going to hold!" shouted Zabeh.

"It has to!" said Ona. But a savage blow smashed the bed frame into her chest and sent her sprawling. She scrambled to her feet and dived back on top of the barricade. A man appeared beside her, one of the injured guards. He had crawled the length of the bunk room to add his weight to the struggle. Another injured guard hobbled over, and several of the refugees came, too.

Then a splintering crack ripped through the room. The barricade sunk into the hatch, dragging Ona with it. She clung to the jumble of timber and saw a hole where the old door had covered the hatch. A face glared up at her. A hand reached through and tore into the bed frame directly beneath her. Ona pushed the frame down, into the demon's face. She spun and kicked and backed away. More splintering and the whole thing lurched again. Someone cried out – one of the injured guards. Ona turned and saw him falling.

The first of the demons battled its way through the splintered pile of wood – a woman whose clothes had been shredded by animal teeth.

Ona scrambled away across the floor. Now she had no choice.

She grabbed Dawn and shook her by the shoulders.

Dawn felt the earth trance slip away as the awful sounds of the bunk room rushed in on her. The circle. She had almost completed the circle. She stared up, disoriented, into Ona's face.

"Look out!" Ona screamed at her.

Dawn looked past her and saw a demon lever itself through the crumpled remains of the hatch. She reached out instinctively and banished it, but another appeared immediately in its place.

Dawn rose to her feet, reaching out and banishing

the next demon, then the next. All around her the other Whisperers woke. Gabriel and Zabeh stood with Ona, ready to fight.

Tuanne was quickly by her side. Then Nara and Alice, too – all joining in the fight. There were still sounds of fighting downstairs, the snarls of Storm and Flame and the battle cries of the guards. Dawn reached through the hatch and banished with such anger and frustration that tears welled in her eyes. She had almost done it! She had almost completed the circle. A minute longer and she could have channelled the earthstone's power.

*Dawn!* cried Ebony, from somewhere outside. *Dawn! Help is coming!*

But what possible help could there be? The Whisperers were all there, or trapped elsewhere, injured, barely surviving.

Then she felt it. A tide of wild, animal power racing towards them.

*Remember the wolves?* said Ebony.

Dawn ran to the window. The animals were coming.

The wolves were the first to arrive, swift and snarling. Dawn watched them crash into the demons. Then more creatures came – stags with antlers that flipped and tore; squat, powerful boar and pouncing wildcats. A bear beat its way into the fray, three times the size of any shape-shifter. A flurry of wings and talons dived in from the skies.

At the hatchway, the demons stopped coming.

"To me!" cried Dawn.

She kneeled again and closed her eyes as the others joined her.

As soon as Dawn reached out, the circle was there. She felt the warmth of greeting, her battle-worn sisters joining together from all across the city.

Ebony hopped on to Dawn's shoulder. *Good luck*, she whispered, and her presence added to the warmth and stability Dawn felt from the circle. The wild creatures had surrounded the barracks, driving the Narlaw away. A strange, deep calm descended.

Dawn took the earthstone in her hands.

Out she pushed, hard and fast. The circle of Whisperers was her raft in an ocean of power. She felt the demons crowding the streets of Meridar and she let the earthstone feed her with its power, let the circle steady her against them.

Dawn reached out into the countryside, into river valleys and rolling hills. Out into the forests, the mountains and the endless southern plains. Her senses spread across the whole of Meridina, gathering force. The earthstone burned inside and all around her.

Now.

Dawn focused on the Narlaw and did what Mika had taught her, tearing into them – every demon, all at once.

The power became pain, but Dawn held on. It screamed through her. Or was it she who was screaming? Time slowed and Dawn felt herself floating, cut loose from everything but the earthstone's terrible power. Her body seemed to melt away. Her thoughts, too. Everything was light and fire. And then, with a deafening surge, the light and the fire and the world itself were torn from her grasp. And a final darkness fell.

Dawn woke, her cheek against the rough floor of the bunk room. She had fallen, passed out, but she didn't know how or when. A breeze came gently though the window and stroked her skin, sweeping loose strands of hair across her eyes. She tried to rise, but her arms and legs felt like tree trunks. She lay facing the wall and her eyes adjusted slowly to the dim light. She heard people moving about behind her. Slow footsteps, low voices. Strange, wild noises outside. But everything seemed blanketed in quiet. It was a quiet she felt deep inside. It was peace.

A shadow fell across her vision. Dawn stretched her eyes wide, but the darkness remained. After a moment of panic, a black beak materialized, bending towards her. Above it was an eye like polished stone.

*It's done*, said Ebony. *The demons are gone.*

Dawn smiled and breathed the sweet night air as if she'd never breathed before.

# CHAPTER 15

There were days when Meridar seemed to shine with its own light. The sky was a glassy blue, and the low autumn sun seemed to gild the yellow sandstone of the city. Dawn rode south on King's Parade, guiding her copper-coloured mare carefully through the bustle. The city was returning to life, rising from the ashes.

Dawn scanned the sky and caught a familiar flash of raven black, low over the rooftops to the south-west. *Can you see her yet?* she whispered.

*No*, replied Ebony, *but there's a crowd near the docks... Wait... It's her. It's the princess. Turn east towards the Fiveways then cut south.*

Dawn wheeled her horse to the right and they clopped into a mid-sized street. The upper floors of the buildings jutted out over Dawn's head, almost meeting in the middle. Most of them were smoke-damaged. A few of them were charred and roofless. People stared as Dawn rode along the strip of sunlight in the centre of the street. She passed a man who was scouring his doorstep with a brush. This was how it should be, Dawn thought. The city returning to normal. Work to be done.

The further south Dawn rode, the worse the damage became. The fighting had been fiercest between King's Parade and the docks. The defenders had held out longer here than anywhere else in the city, and it showed. Whole streets had been reduced to rubble. People clambered over the wreckage, salvaging whatever they could from the remains of their homes.

She could see why Ona had chosen to come to this neighbourhood. It would take a lot of work to make things right here.

*How far?* she asked Ebony.

*Left at the next alley*, said Ebony. *You'll see the crowd.*

Sure enough, Dawn turned the corner and found a throng of people stretching away to the south. The alley echoed with voices, the clack of stone and the creak of ropes. The alley was being cleared of rubble and there was a single neat stack of sandstone blocks, ready to be re-used. People squeezed past Dawn, pushing barrows of rubble, carrying picks and shovels. There was a wagon at the centre of the crowd, stacked with bags of grain that were being handed out. Dawn recognized one of the two young men distributing the food.

"Yusuf!" she called.

He glanced up at her, grinning as he relinquished a sack into someone's outstretched hands. "Dawn!" he called back over the jostling heads. "If you're looking for Ona, she's round at the front. I told her it was time, but she insisted on one more load!"

The crowd parted reluctantly for Dawn's mare and she inched her way through to the front of the wagon.

The princess was sitting on the driver's platform, deep in conversation.

"...And we have space at the palace for more," she was saying. "Just bring them to the gates, or we can send wagons. How many people do you have?"

The talk went back and forth – food, shelter and medicine, questions from both sides. Finally, a grey-haired man strode away from the wagon with a hopeful smile on his face and Ona turned and saw her friend there waiting patiently in her saddle.

"I hate to interrupt your work," said Dawn, "but there's somewhere you have to be today, remember?"

Ona nodded, flashing Dawn a nervous smile. "There are so many people without homes," she said. "I have to do my bit."

"I know," said Dawn. She felt proud of Ona, although she had no right to. This was all Ona's doing. She had outgrown the sheltered life of her childhood and become a woman in her own right, caring and determined.

"I suppose Yusuf can finish off here," said Ona. "If we really must go." She smiled, knowing very well that she was in danger of being late. "Is there room on that saddle for one more?"

"Of course!" said Dawn. She slid forwards as Ona clambered across the driver's platform and slipped on to the saddle behind her and they set off through the swathes of people.

An hour later Dawn was draping the official Palace Whisperer's robe across her shoulders. It was heavy and uncomfortable and the cord that held the robe together dug into the base of Dawn's throat.

*Very fetching*, Ebony commented from her perch high up on a bookshelf in the corner of Dawn's bed chamber. *It's a shame you don't get to wear it more often.*

*It's a shame I don't get to burn it*, Dawn replied, glancing at her purple-clad reflection in the looking glass beside her wardrobe. *It'll have to do*, she muttered. Ebony hopped on to her shoulder as she strode out into the main room of her chambers, smiling as the other Whisperers turned to greet her.

"You look great!" said Nara. "Are you sure it's not you being crowned today?" Flame lay stretched out at Nara's feet, registering Dawn's arrival with a lazy twitch of her ears.

Beside them, Tuanne sat smirking. Nimbus stood up straight on her shoulder as if to get a better look at Dawn.

"I wouldn't want to be crowned, thank you very much," Dawn said, with mock haughtiness. "It's bad enough being the Palace Whisperer – having to put up with this kind of cheek from my Whisperers!"

Alice and Mika joined in with the laughter and Dawn grinned back at them. It was great to be together again. She felt a new closeness towards the Whisperers who had been with her at the final battle. But there had been so much to do since then that Dawn had barely seen any of them. Now, on Ona's coronation day, they had the chance to walk to the ceremony together as guests of honour.

"We should probably go," said Mika, rising slowly from her chair so that Star could jump down from her lap. The little fox stretched and yawned, finding herself side by side with Storm. The huge grey-black wolf looked down at her calmly.

"I think you're right," said Dawn, heading

towards the door. Although she was excited to see Ona crowned queen, she was sad, too. Many of the Whisperers were only staying in Meridar to witness the celebrations. After today, most of them would be heading out across the kingdom, returning home.

In the corridor Dawn walked beside Alice. Storm trotted ahead of them, fearsome and majestic.

"Will you go back to the Great Forest?" Dawn asked.

Alice nodded. "Storm misses the wilderness. And so do I."

"The city's no place for a wolf," said Dawn.

"And the village I'm from," said Alice, "it needs a Whisperer, too. Moraine's decided to stay in the city for a while. She wants to share her healing skills with the infirmary staff here."

"I wish there were more of us," said Dawn.

"There could be more than you think," said Nara from behind them. "Remember where I found Tuanne?"

"Where I found you, more like," said Tuanne.

Nara laughed. "There could be lots of Whisperers

out there, girls and women who never made contact, just them and their companion."

Dawn glanced back at Tuanne and Nimbus. "I'm glad you and Nara found each other," she said.

Tuanne smiled. "Now Nara has to deliver me back to my people," she said. "Otherwise she'll be in more trouble than she's ever known."

"What will you do then?" Dawn asked Nara.

Nara looked thoughtful, uncomfortable even. "I don't know," she said. "My family are farmers. They don't see the use of people like us. Maybe I'll stay with Tuanne for a while. Or maybe travel somewhere new. Coming up here, so far to the north, it's made me realize how big and beautiful the world is. I think I'd like to see it all."

They reached the staircase and wound their way down past the many floors of the Spiral Tower. Dawn noticed how quiet Mika was – more so than usual. She knew Mika had left her mentor behind in the western mountains.

As they descended, the sound of murmuring people gradually became audible, rising up from the parade ground outside. By the time they reached the ground floor, the murmur was almost a roar. Together the Whisperers stepped out into the midday sun. Between the Spiral Tower and the King's Keep a podium had been built, carpeted in luscious red and ornamented with burning braziers and an archway covered in vines and wildflowers. The throne had been positioned in the centre of the podium, magnificently carved and shining with gold leaf. It was flanked by two lesser chairs and behind them stood a row of Guards of the Sun.

More guards were positioned around the podium and the edges of the vast parade ground, along with a great many clerks and officials. The crowd was seated on long rows of benches that stretched back almost to the palace wall. A broad aisle ran through the centre of the crowd, from the palace gate directly to the podium.

Dawn looked around. *I can't see Ona yet*, she said to Ebony. *I hope she turns up.*

*Of course she'll turn up*, said Ebony. *She'll be at Founder's Square, surrounded by her adoring people.*

*Yes*, said Dawn. She felt a flutter of nerves in her stomach, partly on the princess's behalf and partly for herself. One of the seats on the podium was for her.

"Well," said Dawn, "I guess this is where I stop."

Alice hugged her tightly and Ebony leaped into the air, circling above as Alice and Storm headed towards the benches. The front row had been draped with red cloth and reserved for the Whisperers. Dawn noticed a few already in their places – Edie with her bat companion, Katarina with her boar.

Next Dawn hugged Tuanne, feeling Nimbus's thin, curious tail around her own neck for a moment. "I'll see you soon," she said.

Nara hugged her then pulled back and nodded in approval.

Mika smiled as Dawn approached and Dawn wrapped her arms around the young Whisperer's back. "We would never have done it without you," Dawn told her. "I'm proud to be your friend."

"Thank you," whispered Mika. "Me, too."

"You'll be home soon," Dawn said. "You and

Zabeh. You can go and fix things in Rakeen."

Mika nodded.

"But you must promise to come and visit," said Dawn.

"I will," said Mika. She looked around at the blue sky and the light stone buildings that towered over them. "It's not so bad here after all."

Dawn watched as Mika and Star crossed to the front row of benches. Then she made her way into the shade behind the podium. Ebony joined her, primping her feathers as she sat on Dawn's shoulder. Out in the crowd, smartly dressed nobles sat side by side with tradespeople, farmers and palace servants. There had been no tickets or official guest list. Instead, the citizens of Meridar had been invited to queue for a place on the benches, and a line had begun to form well before sunrise, winding for miles away from the palace gates. Those who hadn't secured a seat would stand at the back and all around, but it was tradition that they should follow the new monarch from Founder's Square, or fall in behind her procession as she rode.

The new monarch. Dawn still couldn't quite believe Princess Ona's coronation had come so soon. She glanced across at the heavily guarded entrance to the King's Keep. Inside, King Eneron would be preparing himself for the ceremony, too. Dawn saw a flash of green in the shadowed entrance and recognized Lady Tremaine, elegant as always in a long emerald dress.

*What a shame Ona won't be requiring the warden's services*, Ebony said.

Lady Tremaine had opposed Dawn at every step, endangering the kingdom many times out of pride and stupidity. Now Ona had forbidden her to work in the palace after her coronation and Dawn couldn't help but feel pleased about that.

A heightening in the noise of the crowd drew Dawn's attention to the palace gate.

*I think they're coming*, she said.

A grey-clad palace official hurried over to Dawn with confirmation. "This way, please," he said, ushering her towards the podium.

*Make sure you smile*, said Ebony.

*I hope you've groomed your feathers properly*, Dawn replied, stepping up on to the thick red carpet of the podium. She lowered herself into the chair to the left of the throne and saw King Eneron ascend the steps at the other side of the stage. He nodded at Dawn as he took the chair on that side and Dawn nodded back respectfully. It must have been a hard decision, handing the throne over to his daughter. But it was the right one, and Dawn was thankful for it.

Dawn peered through the palace gate and on to the King's Parade. People thronged the sides of the avenue and, in the far distance, a banner flapped in the wind.

The procession grew closer. She could see the standard-bearer clearly now, riding at the head of the line on a horse dressed in the same red and gold finery as its rider. The flag of Meridina hung above them, a golden sun on red and blue quarters, gold braid and tassels at its edges. Cheers went up as the princess climbed the gentle hill towards the Palace of the Sun, but Dawn couldn't see her yet. She glanced across the front row of the crowd, smiling at her friends, then she saw another familiar face grinning up at her.

Gabriel – with Titus perched politely where his hands lay crossed in his lap. He winked at Dawn and his grin broadened.

Dawn couldn't help but smile back. Seeing him there at the front of the crowd, she wondered again whether he would stay in Meridar or travel back to his home in the western mountains. Secretly, she hoped very much that he would stay.

The procession reached the gates and two flanks of buglers stepped forwards to blast a fanfare that sent a flock of starlings flapping into the sky. The standard-bearer rode through the tall arch of the palace gate and Dawn felt another swift flutter of nerves. But as the flag of Meridina bobbed to the side and Princess Ona rode into view, Dawn's nerves were swept away by pride and happiness and hope.

There she was, upright and beautiful in her coronation gown. Behind her, as she rode, was the whole of Meridar. The people spilled out to the left and right, filling the vast parade ground. Another fanfare shot into the air and the standard-bearer bellowed, "All rise for Ona, Princess of Meridina!"

The parade ground thundered with applause. Confetti burst from the standing crowds as Ona passed, slow and stately, down the aisle. Behind the princess strode a pair of palace guards – Captain Valderin and a woman with one arm, her blue cloak rising in the breeze. Dawn thought briefly of Loren and all the others who had not made it through. It was her duty, and the duty of everyone who had survived, to cherish their memories, to make Meridina whole again, to protect the wilds from anything that might threaten them.

Ona had reached the podium, her gold dress shimmering beneath a cloak of deepest red. Dawn caught her eye and they shared a nervous smile. Here was the queen Meridina had been waiting for. Here was Ona, her friend.

# ABOUT THE AUTHOR

Kris Humphrey grew up in Plymouth,
where he spent most of his time reading books,
riding around on his bike and daydreaming
about writing a book himself. Since then,
Kris has had more jobs than he cares to think
about. He has been a cinema projectionist, a
bookseller and worked at an animal sanctuary
in the Guatemalan jungle.

*A Whisper of Wolves*, the first book in
the Guardians of the Wild series,
was Kris's first novel.